Two Rode From Texas

Fleeing back to Texas after a gun-wrangle had gone wrong, Wade Prescott and his partner, Jim Langford, soon find themselves in even greater trouble. Before they know it, they're mixed up in a bloody range war – and fighting on opposing sides.

However, a brutal assault brings the two friends side-by-side again for a last deadly showdown with a ruthless rancher and his violent henchmen.

Two rode from Texas and two would return – but dead or alive?

Two Rode from Texas

Frank Longfellow

BRACKNELL FOREST
BOROUGH COUNCIL

A Black Horse Western

ROBERT HALE · LONDON

BBRA		BCRO	
BASH		BGRE	
BBIN	ı\14	BHAR	
BBIR		BSAN	
RCON		BWHI	

Typeset by
Derek Doyle & Associates, Shaw Heath.
Printed and bound in Great Britain by
Antony Rowe Limited, Wiltshire.

*To Des, Michael and all my friends in
the City of the Tribes*

CHAPTER 1

As soon as he entered the crowded, smoke-filled interior of the room, Wade savvied something was amiss. But then it didn't take much brains to figure that out. The whole saloon seemed frozen like a frame of that new-fangled invention, the camera. Glasses were gripped motionless in white-knuckled fists and, without realizing it, every customer in the bar was holding his breath in spellbound anticipation. Cigar smoke curled lazily upward in the still atmosphere while somewhere a blowfly buzzed on oblivious, amazingly loud in that well of silence.

All eyes were riveted compulsively on the two figures facing each other at opposite ends of the floor, one a dark-clad, thin and vicious-looking man with venom written in his eyes, whose claw-like hand was hovering over the butt of his ivory-plated pistol. The other was a gangling fair-haired youth with a shabby gunbelt and holster that had a borrowed look about them. His face was ghastly white with fear and his hand trembled above his weapon, but mingled, too, with the foreboding on his features, was an underlying expression of defiance and determination, a quality the old-timers aptly called grit. But from the evident poise and professional demeanour of his adversary, there could be little doubt which of the two would come out of the encounter alive.

The Texan took in the situation at a glance and, without a second's hesitation, strode up to the bar-counter, putting himself directly in the line of fire of the two would-be duellists. He slapped the polished mahogany with the flat of his hand.

'Whiskey, barman, and make it pronto. I got me a real trail thirst.'

The tender seemed at first too frightened to budge, but at Wade's repeated command, he sprang to produce a bottle and tumbler, all the while eyeing the pair of protagonists whose game the stranger had so dangerously interrupted. Wade poured himself a generous measure of the amber fluid set before him and drank it off at a toss. He gave a sigh of satisfaction and, refilling the glass for a more leisurely enjoyment, he half-turned idly to survey his surroundings, the picture of a man utterly at peace with the world.

A low murmur of speculation went around the crowd: was Wade mad? Or just stupid? Couldn't he see what was afoot? How would Bud Lewis react? For this was the name of the thin, dark man whose stance and air bespoke one whose trade was killing.

They didn't have long to wait for the answer to the

last question. When he had recovered from the initial surprise of this unexpected interruption, Lewis aimed a cold and terse request to Wade.

'Mister, why don't you take a seat? Me and this farm-boy gotta little unfinished business to take care of and you're standing in a mighty unhealthy position right now.'

Wade draped an elbow on the bar and turned to face the other man full on.

'*Amigo*, I always drink at the bar. Get to meet more folks that way. Have a friendly word or two when they're orderin' in their drinks. Don't see no reason to change the habit of a lifetime now.'

Lewis's eyes narrowed in fury and his fingers twitched impulsively over his revolver. But all the time the detached, professional side of his mind was working non-stop. He'd be paid no fee for killing this meddlesome stranger; it would only make for more trouble with the law, such as it was. Besides, though he didn't like to admit it himself, this *hombre* with the smiling mouth but hard eyes seemed like someone who might have seen his own share of gunplay. His gaze flickered over the rig of the man facing him. The holster was low-slung and securely tied to the thigh with a leather thong. The pistol looked like it had been filed at the hammer and sight for swifter draw and more rapid fire. The weapon had a deadly, well-cared-for appearance, as if its owner made regular use of it – and not for driving staples on a bobwire fence either. All in all the risk was too great. He could take the kid any time he liked. Time was on his side.

He licked his lips and sneered unpleasantly at Wade.

'All right, mister. If you want to wet-nurse this greenhorn, go right ahead. You can't always be around to hold his hand. He'll keep until another day.'

He threw back his drink and, casting an evil glance at the other clientele, shoved his way through them into the street.

Immediately the whole room drew one unconscious sigh of relief and several of the men gathered round Wade, vying with noisy offers to buy him a drink.

Into this throng came another man, also a stranger to the place, who elbowed his way among the back-slappers to the object of their enthusiastic congratulations.

He looked puzzled and a little annoyed at the adulation the Texan at the bar was receiving as he addressed him with the rough familiarity of a trail partner.

'Hell's bells, Wade, what've you done now? Tell these folks the railroad's a'comin' through, or their town's sittin' on a gold mine or somethin'?'

Wade turned his cool ironic blue eyes on his friend.

'Nope. All I did was order me a drink and folks seem to think that makes me some kind of hero.'

The older man regarded Wade with a searching stare. He knew his *compadre* would never tell a lie but sometimes he had a mighty peculiar way of telling the truth. Only by dogged questioning could the full story be dragged out of the close-mouthed cowboy, and right now he just couldn't be bothered. He'd just come from leaving their animals at the livery stable after a long ride in the burning sun and all he wanted right now was a long cool drink, not some fool mystery to perplex his pounding head.

Wade forestalled his next move by ordering him a beer, which the barman refused to take any payment for. That lightened his companion's mood a little, but not much. He took a thirsty swig of it and turned to Wade with a gloomy air.

'I've just been talking to the stableman. He can put us in his barn for the night. But he can't guarantee us any sleep. It's end of the month payday for the rannies in these parts and there'll be drunks staggerin' in at all hours. Might as well try and get forty winks in New York Central Station as in there tonight.'

The younger man pulled a face.

'Ain't there some kind of hotel or rooming-house in this no-account burg?'

'Nope, no rooming-house and the hotel is booked out. Some cowboys like a nice feather bed after a hard night's carousin'.'

'Heck, Jim, ain't there even a place we can eat? I'm so hungry right now I could swallow a whole steer,

11

horns, hoofs and hide.'

The older man scratched his jaw pensively.

'Well, as regards that, I ain't got to lookin' yet. There's got to be some kind of establishment in town where a man don't risk getting gut-ache.'

'Don't count on it, mister,' chirped in the bartender, who had been listening with half an ear cocked, whilst ostensibly polishing glasses. 'Only restaurant around here is a *cantina* run by a Mex name of Pedro. If you like your food with plenty of oil and don't care overmuch 'bout its freshness, that's the place for you. Greasers eat there a lot,' – he spat contemptuously into the sawdust on the floor – 'but nary a white man.'

Wade and Jim exchanged a look of dismay. Things were getting worse and worse. No food, no sleep – what *could* this benighted spot offer them? Harrisville was the next nearest town and it was a good three-hour ride and not even on their route. With both their horses tuckered out and their riders in not much better shape, the idea of moving on to another town at this hour of the day did not appeal to the weary duo.

But luckily their saviour was at hand. The youth whose life Wade had so bravely saved but whom he had thereafter ignored, had been hovering around the vicinity of the two partners with growing excitement and he now burst in eagerly with an unexpected offer.

'Look here, gents, I know a place where you can

get a good square meal and a roof over your head and it won't cost a cent.'

Wade eyed the kid dubiously.

'You do? Where?'

'At our farm,' replied the youngster, seemingly delighted at the brilliant solution to their problem. 'There's plenty of room in our barn and my sis is about the best cook this side of the county. She just baked a fresh batch of scones this morning and there's plenty of dried beef in the larder. It's just a matter of throwing a few more hunks of it into the stew-pot and you'll have as fine a meal as you've ever tasted.'

He finished with a beaming, expectant smile and the two friends looked at each other questioningly.

'Thanks just the same, kid, but I don't cotton to spending the night under a sodbuster's roof. I'm a cattleman through and through and it wouldn't sit right with me to be beholden to a dirt-farmer.'

It was Jim who spoke these words and, despite an effort to put a dally on the harshness of his reply, the bitterness and resentment that every rangeman felt towards the folk who fenced in and ploughed up his beloved prairie burned through like a fiery brand. Yet Jim Langford was not a vindictive or mean-spirited man. It was his very love of the beauty and wildness of the grassy plains of his homeland that caused him to feel deep rancour towards those whom he saw as destroying it.

The face of the youth dropped piteously before

this stern rebuff and the bright grin vanished from his features like a candle doused by the wind.

Either because of this, or else through more self-interested motives, Wade spoke up in a more conciliatory tone.

'Now hold on a minute, Jim. This young fella's just aimin' to be friendly. No need to growl at him like a grizzly with a toothache. The way I see it, we ain't got no choice 'cept to take up his kind offer. I don't fix to spend the whole night listenin' to my rumblin' belly or a choir of snorin' drunks. You can suit yourself, but I aim to go with this feller and accept his hospitality.'

Langford regarded his companion with hard, fathoming eyes, and for a moment there was tenseness in the air. Then he relaxed and his natural good humour came flooding back into his countenance.

'Guess you're right, Wade. A bed's a bed and a bite's a bite, no matter who's offerin'.'

He turned to the young farmer.

'OK, kid, lead on. I didn't mean anything personal by what I said, but the fact is, that though I'm goin' along with this, we're both on different sides of the fence. And I ain't forgettin' that it was you and your kind that put the damn fence there in the first place!'

CHAPTER 2

The ride out to Seth Anderson's place, for that was the boy's name, was not a comfortable one. Wade was his usual jovial self and chatted merrily with their young companion, who responded with adolescent awkwardness to the cowboy's friendly banter. As well as his inexperience in dealing with other people, the lad had a serious and overly adult view of life. The hardship of running a homestead and earning a living at so young an age seemed to have squeezed all the natural sprightliness of spirit from him. His reply to Wade's small talk and questions about his farm and his sister showed a heaviness and humourlessness that was out of place in someone of his age.

But occasionally a half-reluctant smile lit his features as Wade's ready wit found its mark. The cowboy felt sorry for the boy and went out of his way to draw him out about his hopes and plans for the future. He knew how it was with the kid for, like him, he too had been orphaned at an early age and realized from bitter experience how hard it was to make one's way in the world without the tender comfort and support of loving parents.

As regards Jim, he plodded on behind in taciturn silence. As so often before, he was falling in with Wade's wayward moods, but that didn't mean to say he liked it. It went against his grain to bunk down under a sodbuster's roof and he wasn't about to pretend otherwise. He had fixed in his mind that he and his partner would push on at first light the next day, come hell or high water, no matter how pretty the boy's sister was, or how much a breakfast of farm-fresh eggs and home-cured ham might tempt a cowboy's appetite. But on top of all this, Jim smelled trouble in this valley like the dense sulphur-charged air that preceded a thunderstorm. He'd smelled it before in a dozen different places and always – when the trouble finally broke – it was followed by mayhem and death. In the old days, the brooding sense of impending danger had enthralled and attracted him. But now he was getting a mite older and a mite more cautious. It was funny how, as the years advanced ever nearer to the moment of dissolution, the more precious the gift of life seemed to grow. Time was when Jim would have risked his hide for a saloon-girl's smile or a foolish bet, but those days were gone and a wiser man now strode the saddle of that cowboy's bronc.

After a few efforts to cajole his trail buddy into joining the conversation, Wade gave up on him and decided to let the stubborn old cuss stew in his own saturnine juice. For his part, he reckoned the chance of pleasant lodgings and a good filling meal was too tempting a prospect to turn down and he'd accept a deal like that from the Devil himself, should that gent make so kind as to offer the same.

Before long they topped a ridge and spied a rectangle of light from a house somewhere in the blue dusk gathering around them.

Seth turned to them, his eyes shining with pride and excitement.

'That's it. That's our place yonder. Nicest piece of land you ever seen, bar none.'

Wade looked at the boy. His face was transformed by the joy of ownership and belonging. And somehow he seemed to loom larger in the fading light, seemed here on his home ground more a man than a boy.

'Well, let's get on then,' growled Jim impatiently. 'It weren't my idea to come along, but now we're here, let's ride on in 'stead of gawkin' at it like kids at a cookie-jar.'

He spurred his horse down the slope, his annoyance showing by the sharp kick he gave his normally well-trained animal, as if he was in a hurry to get an unpleasant experience well and truly over with.

When they got to the house, Seth dismounted quickly and led the way in, calling out to his sister as he did so. Wade and Jim, following more tentatively, found themselves in a simple but clean and well-lit room, sparse of furniture but cosy and welcoming with a potbelly stove in one corner and the mouth-

watering smell of stew wafting through the air.
Standing over a cooking-pot, with her face still
flushed from the heat of the oven, stood a slim, dark-
haired girl who looked at them in surprise. The
Texans hastily removed their hats and Seth stepped
forward to make the necessary introductions.

'Rachel, this is Wade Prescott and his friend Jim
Langford. Wade showed up in the saloon when Bud
Lewis was trying to force me into a drawing match
and faced him down – right in front of everybody.
You should have seen it!'

Rachel's reaction to this blurted explanation of
the presence of the two strangers in her living-room
took the men a little off-guard.

'And what were you doing in the saloon, Seth
Anderson? Haven't I asked you a hundred times not
to go there? You're too young to be frequenting a
place like that and besides, you know that Bud Lewis
and his sort are always hanging around there, just
waiting to start trouble. You're only making it easy for
them by what you do.'

Seth lowered his eyes sulkily at this reproach.

'I'm old enough to go anywhere I want. And
anyway, Lewis and his kind don't scare me. I'll go up
against him any day of the week.'

'Yes and that's what he's counting on. Can't you
see that you're playing right into his hands this way?
Why can't you stay clear of him and his friends? It can
only end in one way – and you know what that is.'

Wade and Jim exchanged a questioning glance.

Despite the small gap in years between this boy who was in his late teens and his sister who was in her early twenties, it was obvious that there was a bigger difference in maturity. Rachel behaved more like a mother than a sister and they felt awkward and intrusive as Seth got this tongue-lashing from his irate kinswoman.

Rachel must have read their embarrassment for she suddenly broke off her confrontation with her brother and turned her attention to them with an apologetic smile.

'I'm sorry, gentlemen, but my brother has a habit of getting himself into trouble and thereby dragging innocent folk like yourselves into the situation. You'll have to excuse him. Please join us for dinner, which I imagine is the reason Seth's brought you all the way out here. It's the least we can do to repay your help.'

'I don't know about being "innocent folk",' chuckled Wade, 'but I was happy to help Seth out. We all need a little hand now and again. Could be he'll be around next time to pull *me* out of a scrape.'

Seth coloured with pleasure at the idea that he could be of assistance to this tough rangeman, who was already something of a hero in his eyes. Rachel noticed it and liked the modest way the stranger had shrugged off the debt of gratitude rightly owed him by this clever compliment.

'Well,' she said, 'if you men would like to clean up some after your journey, food'll be ready in just a little while.'

Seth took them to a pump out the back where they doused off the sweat and dust of a day's riding with some cold well water. Then he showed them the barn where they would be spending the night. The place was warm and dry and smelt of sweet grass. After they tended their horses and stalled them for the night, Wade flopped down on the soft hay piled high in the grange.

'What say, pard?' he grinned at Jim. 'Sorry you came now? Don't this beat any fancy four-corner feather bed?'

Jim allowed himself a grunt of approval.

'I reckon so. But I still want to be on our way first thing. The sooner we reach Texas, the happier I'll be.'

'As regards that,' said Wade, chewing a stalk of grass thoughtfully. 'I ain't in no particular hurry. I don't know if you noticed, but that girl is mighty pretty. Could be she might be able to use a hand around here for a day or two. Wouldn't harm to rest up the horses before we hit the trail again. Fact is, I wouldn't mind a spell of home-cookin' and some good-lookin' female company neither. No harm to you, Jim, but I'm plumb tired of seein' nothin' but that ugly mug of your'n day after day.'

Wade's teasing banter failed to take a rise out of the older man. Jim was too well acquainted with his friend's ways by now to be taken in by his mischievous sense of humour. He knew that Wade was as anxious to get back to Texas as he was and no woman, however pleasant or comely, would delay the home-sick cowboy.

'Sure, sure,' he muttered, as he pulled a blanket from his saddle-bag. 'I'll try not to wake you up in the mornin' when I go and I'll tell them in Texas not to start the celebrations for your home-comin' just yet.'

The dour cowboy was not devoid of his own brand of sarcastic wit.

Just then Seth arrived with the news that their meal was ready and the two friends eagerly followed the aroma of beef stew to the table of their hosts. Even Jim had to admit it: the meal was a good one. The stew was simple but delicious and was followed by freshly ground coffee and the scones Seth had bragged about. His boasts turned out to be justified and Rachel watched, amused, as the two visitors wolfed down a half-dozen each before looking in embarrassed surprise at the empty plate before them.

'I guess you gentlemen must have been a mite hungry,' she declared with humorous irony.

Wade grinned back. 'Reckon you're lucky we didn't eat the plate and all, Rachel.'

By now the pair were on first name terms, much to Jim's discomfort, and already there seemed to be a lot unspoken between them. Wade even insisted on helping to clear up the dishes whilst Seth, suddenly exhausted by the delayed impact of the day's events, retired early to bed. Jim sat at the table sleepily, savouring a glass of well-mellowed whiskey from an earthenware jug that Rachel had produced at the end of the meal. He knew that, save for his presence, the conversation between the young pair merrily chatting amidst the pots and pans at the washtub might take a dangerously personal tone and he was determined to prevent that. Soon the washing-up was done and the conversation languished, cramped by the heavy company of the older man. Wade realized that his trail buddy wasn't about to leave the room without him, so he bade a wistful farewell to his winsome hostess and walked to the barn with Jim. The pair hadn't much to say to each other except a gruff goodnight as they rolled themselves up in their blankets and snuggled down in the soft hay. Only one peculiarity marked out their bedtime ritual from that of any other cowpoke bedding down for the night under a prairie sky. Without any thought about it, each from habit placed his gun under the rolled up slicker that served as a pillow, so as to be within easy reach in the dark, and each set close to hand his saddle-bag with a back-up weapon in it. Too many of their friends and enemies had died from not having a revolver close by at a critical moment or from having no second chance at survival if the first gun should jam. But the hearty meal, the warming whiskey and the day's exertions quickly wrought their effect and the men fell immediately into a deep and dreamless sleep.

*

The riders came out of the east, descending the purple slopes of sage with grim and silent purpose. All the jokey, whiskey-inspired jossing had ceased and now the men and horses pushed forward in steady, relentless motion. There were around ten or twelve of them, mostly muffled against the early morning chill, their faces white and phantom-like in the dim light and set in an expression of implacable ruthlessness. As they neared the sleeping ranch house, they paused simultaneously and drew up on the ridge overlooking the scatter of buildings, staring down on it as a hungry wolf might survey its prey.

For a few moments no words were spoken. Each of the men fingered his six-gun nervously, testing its readiness to draw. A few drew out carbines from their sheaths, with the soft slither of steel against leather sounding unnaturally loud in the stillness of the night. For some seconds there was total quiet as they awaited the word from their leader that would send them charging down the rise at a furious gallop to the defenceless homestead below.

Savouring his power, his ability to unleash the mayhem that would follow, the leader delayed the fatal command as long as he could. In the taut silence, only the breathing of the men could be heard, along with an impatient nicker from one of the animals. Finally the head-rider spoke, his voice a harsh, rasping whisper.

'Remember what the boss said you fellers, kill the kid if he gets in the way, but don't harm the woman.'

With this curt and pregnant reminder, he sank his spurs into the side of his bronc and took off down the hill with a bloodcurdling yell. The other cowboys weren't long in following suit and the place rang out with their hollers and yips like Dodge City at a drive's end. To add to the excitement and uproar, the men loosed off shots into the air while their horses bucked and snorted in maddened frenzy. It might have seemed to any casual observer like a piece of rough range horseplay, such as was common among the fraternity of western cattle herders. But then a red flare ignited the darkness and sailed through the air to land on the roof of a barn, smashing to spread out in greedy tongues of fire. Another and another of these incendiaries appeared in the night and burst into fiery blossom upon the wooden structures of the outbuildings. The wild cries of the raiders increased as the timber caught light and threw up billows of black smoke and blazing sparks. It all seemed like a scene from some hellish nightmare, with prancing demons lit by the flickering glare of infernal flames.

Then four guns spoke and sent a salvo of destruction into the milling pack of attackers. Immediately, one tumbled from his saddle as if swatted by a giant, invisible hand. Another clutched his leg with an agonized oath. The others stopped in their tracks and looked at each other in amazed conjecture. Someone in the burning building was shooting at them with some heavy and deadly accurate artillery. They hadn't reckoned on that; burning out a woman

24

and her kid brother was one thing, trading lead with hidden gunsharps was quite another. For a second the question hung in the air like the smoke around them: should they fight or run? Another hail of shots tore several Stetsons from their owners' heads. Hell's bells, the *hombres* in the barn were only playing with them! They could just as easily put those bullets through their hearts as through their hats! The cowardly gang needed no further encouragement and lit out at full tilt, only a few daring to twist in the saddle and trigger off a couple of wildly inaccurate parting rounds.

As the sound of retreating hoof beats faded, two figures emerged from the smoke, guns in both hands, and warily surveyed the scene around them.

'Looks like they're all gone,' ventured Wade.

' 'Cept for him,' replied Jim, nodding in the direction of the crumpled body of the raider who had caught some of the flying lead.

It was pretty obvious to them both that the man was dead but they advanced towards him to confirm this grisly fact. Bending down, Wade tugged away the bandanna which half-covered the face of the corpse and started in recognition at the sight he beheld.

'It's that jasper from the saloon today,' he explained to Jim. 'What was his name? . . . Bud Lewis. I'll bet he was in charge of that bunch of coyotes. Well, I reckon his bullying days are over now.'

Just then Rachel and Seth came rushing up.

'Are you all right?' she demanded anxiously. 'Is

anyone hurt? I got Seth down to the cellar as soon as the attack began. I didn't want him risking his life against a gang of ruffians like that.'

'Aw, I would've been OK,' insisted Seth peevishly. 'I coulda give as good as I got.'

'Your sis was right,' said Wade grimly. 'They would've been expecting trouble from the house and they had it covered. We hit them from the barn, took them off-guard.'

Suddenly Seth noticed the figure on the ground.

'Say, did you get one of them?' he asked excitedly.

Hurriedly, Wade replaced the bandanna over the gaping visage of the fallen gunslinger. Death was never pretty, and a violent end was the ugliest kind of all.

'Yeah,' he said curtly, 'but he ain't goin' anywhere, so we'll take care of him in the morning. Meantime let's put out these fires before they get worse.'

Without the feeding hand of the arsonists, the flames were raging less avidly now and some determined dousing with several buckets of water brought the conflagration under control.

'Best get some sleep now,' Wade ordered the Andersons when the blaze had finally been extinguished. 'I don't think those varmints will be back in a hurry, but Jim and I will stand guard until dawn just in case.'

The brother and sister obeyed meekly; in a situation like this, a man such as Wade was to be listened to, for somehow he seemed to be in his element in a crisis, as if it was part of his normal, everyday existence.

Wade and Jim flipped a coin for the first watch which the younger man won, so after washing off his smoke-begrimed face at the water-pump, he grabbed some hay from the partly burnt barn, spread it on the porch of the house and threw himself on to it. It wasn't long before he was fast asleep again, despite the bitter, acrid smell of woodsmoke that still seemed to fill his aching head.

CHAPTER 3

Breakfast the next morning was a sombre affair. The two men had loaded Lewis's body on to one of the farm horses to bring it into town for burial and cleared up some of the debris caused by the raid. But the place was still a charred and smoky shambles. It would need a lot of work to set it right again.

Rachel explained to the Texans the background to the dispute – an all-too-familiar story of homesteaders against cattlemen, in this case one particular cattleman called Morgan King, who ran the Red Sun ranch, the biggest in the territory. Beef prices were at an all-time high and King was keen to extend his range by any means he could, fair or foul. Trouble had been brewing for a long while, with mostly petty acts of harassment. But with the recent hiring of Bud Lewis, the ante had been raised considerably and now things looked set to boil right over.

'Why don't you just up and leave?' asked Wade. 'There's plenty of other places you could make a go of, without gun-totin' visitors droppin' by in the dead of night.'

Rachel looked at him hard-eyed.

'In the first place no one's interested in taking this place. They know they'd be buying themselves into a range war. Only King's in the market and he's offering barely half what the land's worth. He knows I'm over a barrel and he owns the barrel. And in the second place, even if he made a fair offer, I still wouldn't give him the satisfaction of running me off. We come from fighting stock and we don't give in to blackmail and violence. The homesteaders in this area will have to stick together, otherwise King will take over the whole caboodle.'

'Lady,' interposed Jim with a long-suffering sigh, 'you got more sand than sense. King already has this valley in his pocket. Where were your farmer friends last night when the lead started flyin'? The nearest one's only a fifteen-minute ride from here but I didn't see no neighbours dashing to the rescue. They was all quakin' under their sheets and prayin' to God they wouldn't be next. They're ploughmen, not pistoleros. If it wasn't for us, this bacon we're eatin' right now would have been cooked hours ago along with everything else, includin' maybe yourselves.'

The girl turned pale at this brutal assessment of the facts and Wade shot an admonishing glance at his partner. Everything Jim had said was true but there was no need to state it in such forthright terms. Rachel had got a bad enough fright without it, despite her plucky spirit, and Jim was only rubbing salt in the wounds with his accurate but blunt summing-up of the situation.

'Haven't you any kinfolk you can call on to help you defend the place, at least until the trouble blows over?' he asked gently, trying to make up for his *compadre*'s gruffness.

'No,' replied the girl, with a tearful, hunted look entering her eyes. 'There's just me and Seth. All our other folks are dead and gone.'

'Well,' said Jim, to break the slightly awkward silence that ensued, 'I reckon it's time for us to push on. We're mighty obliged for your hospitality and I hope you get your problems sorted out by and by.'

'Yes,' replied Rachel, forcing a smile. 'And I must thank you for all your help. I'll wake up Seth to say goodbye. I let him sleep on a little today – he was exhausted after all the excitement and hullabaloo of last night.'

Jim got up and strode purposefully towards the door but Wade dawdled a while, thoughtfully swirling the dregs of his coffee before tossing back the cup and following in his companion's footsteps. It was obvious that he wasn't just as clear-cut in his mind about their plans as Jim appeared to be. When he reached the barn he found his friend already saddling up his mount.

Making no attempt to go for his own gear, he took out the makings and commenced to roll himself a cigarette, as if playing for time in which to make a decision. Jim pressed on regardless, ignoring Wade's hovering presence.

'Seems to me these folk could do with a hand,' Wade finally ventured.

'Ain't none of our business,' stated Jim flatly, carrying on with his packing.

'Maybe it should be,' came the reply.

'Tarnation!' exploded Jim, throwing his saddlebags to the ground. 'I knowed it would come to this. I knowed you couldn't resist some wet-nosed kid and his big-eyed sister.'

He suddenly stopped, took a deep breath and continued more calmly, 'Listen Wade, these are farmers against cattlemen. We're cattlemen, remember? If anything, we should be working for King, not them.'

'As regards that,' replied Wade hotly, 'we ain't rannies no more. We gave that up, your idea. Second, remember what happened last time we sided with cattlemen against settlers? A fine mess that turned out to be!'

'You're blamin' me for that, boy?' growled the older man, now thoroughly beside himself with anger. 'It was our one chance to better ourselves and I let you in on it so you could make good. Was that my fault?'

'Yeah, but look at the way it turned out. It wasn't anything like you said. Not at all.'

The two men glowered at each other but as their hostile looks locked, each saw in the other's face an ugly reflection of his own expression of enmity and anger and gradually the gaze of both faltered and fell to the ground.

31

Suddenly the older man stepped up on to his horse.

'I'm takin' the body of the man we killed last night into town to let the sheriff know what happened,' he said. 'Providin' he accepts my story, I'll be on my way by noon. If you want to ride with me, you'll find me at the saloon.'

Wade made no reply but just continued to stare at the ground, his brow knitted in a stubborn frown. After a few seconds' hesitation, Jim wheeled round his horse and spurred it away with a dig of his heels, hardly pausing to snatch up the reins of the animal bearing the grisly casualty of the previous night's shoot-out.

Wade watched him disappear into the distance, biting his lip in an agony of indecision. Should he go after his partner and apologize? Try to persuade him to stay? It wouldn't do any good though, for the older man's opposition to farmers was implacable and they could all fry in Hell before he would lift a finger to help them. On the other hand, Wade wasn't about to abandon a helpless girl to the clutches of an unscrupulous ruffian on account of his *compadre*'s deep-seated prejudices.

His reveries were interrupted by a gentle query.

'Did you have an argument with your friend, Wade?'

Rachel stood framed in the doorway of the barn, nervously twisting a kitchen towel in her hands. It was obvious that she sensed the acrimonious atmosphere that still hung in the air after Jim's precipitate departure. Wade looked hard at her. She'd probably guessed that she was the cause of the rupture between him and his partner and was waiting to see if he was about to join him. He could read fear and, at the same time, timorous hope in her eyes and his resolve suddenly hardened.

'Yeah,' he replied. 'He's movin' on but I figger to stick around — if you can use a hand to put this place together again.'

Relief flooded her face and she surged forward towards him in gratitude, as if she were about to throw herself into his arms. But, at the last moment, she recollected herself and stopped, smiling in flustered delight.

But Wade was in a more sombre set of mind. He knew he'd made the right decision by the girl's happy reaction, but he still felt a heaviness in his heart that his long friendship with Jim had ended in such sorry circumstances. He kept silent for a moment or two while the excited girl waited expectantly for him to lay out his plans. But Wade's mind seemed elsewhere. When he looked at her again she could see sadness and regret in his eyes and her spirits sank a little as she saw how troubled the cowboy was at his difficult decision.

'I want you to understand something, Rachel,' he began earnestly. 'I ain't trying to excuse Jim but I want you to know why he's actin' the way he is. It ain't out of hate but out of love. He was raised up in the wild of the prairie and was ridin' wild horses bare-back across the plains nearly before he could walk. That kind of freedom, ridin' full gallop over the grassland, with the wind in your face and nothin' 'tween you and the skyline except miles of open country, it gets in a man's blood. Once they started putting up barbed-wire fences and quartering up the land into homesteads, it was like they were cutting up his heart too and selling it off to the highest bidder. He don't see that things have to change and that the West can't stay wild and free, the way it always was.'

Wade gave a bitter laugh.

'Can't say I'm dead struck on the notion either, but there ain't nothin' we can do about it. Times change and people have to change with them.'

Rachel rested her hand on Wade's arm, a look of understanding on her face.

'I think I know what you're saying. It seems we can't make a step of progress without losing some-thing precious and good along with it.'

Wade glanced at her.

'Sure,' he said shortly, and shook off her friendly hold. At the moment he was still hurting from the break-up of a close friendship and the comfort of a comparative stranger, however well-meaning, was not yet welcome.

'I think I'll scout around some to see if there's any sign of those varmints from last night,' he said abruptly. 'It's not likely but they may have left a man to keep a watch on the place to see what's goin' on.'

Rachel looked at him searchingly, then let her gaze drop. She realized that her sympathy was a little premature, that Wade needed some time alone to adjust to his loss and that this move was just a gambit to gain him that time.

'Fine,' she said. 'If you're back around midday I'll have food ready on the table. Meantime Seth and I will get on with fixing the damage from the raid.'

As soon as Wade got on his horse and cantered out of the yard, he felt a sight better. Somehow the familiar swaying of the animal under him, the creak of saddle leather and the steady rhythm of hoofbeats soothed like an old forgotten lullaby.

'Reckon it reminds me of better times,' he reflected.

But this brought his thoughts back to his trail-partner of long standing and gloom settled on him again. After a while he came to a rock pool clustered round with pine and oak and fed by a bubbling stream. Drawn by the prettiness of the spot, he dismounted and tethered his horse. Then he perched himself on a boulder, idly scooped up a handful of pebbles and began to plop them into the still, smooth surface of the water as he tried to order his tangled feelings from the turbulent events of the past few hours.

Like most men of action, Wade was not accustomed to dealing with his emotions. In his line there weren't usually too many emotions to deal with. There were few women in his world, no children – just partners. But the bond between partners was a strong, enduring one; it was built on mutual hard-ship, occasional danger, but mainly formed by the humdrum routine of everyday existence. It was like an old pair of boots that had worn soft and pliable with years of use, that had moulded themselves to every contour and peculiarity of the feet – that were so comfortable and broke-in that you forgot you were wearing them at all. But come the day you had to throw them away, you realized what a sorely missed item they would be.

Now as Wade pitched stones into the mirror-like pond and watched the ripples he created grow and die out, he felt that somehow, without his willing it, big changes were happening in his own life.

For a start there was the woman. She was sure enough pretty but he'd seen prettier, kissed them and rode away without so much as a backward glance. But this time it was different; Rachel was alone and vulnerable. She needed his protection and, somehow, this gave her a hold over him that none of the others had. In this case his own strength had become his weakness for it made him respon-sible: his conscience would not permit him to leave this girl and her kid brother to their doom.

But he had wrecked his friendship with Jim by the course he'd chosen to follow. Faced by the same situ-ation, Jim had chosen to walk away from it. Perhaps his buddy had more sense than he had. They'd had some good times together. They'd shared the laugh-ter, the whiskey, the women, the cold, the heat, the trail-dust and the bitter tang of camp-fire coffee. Perhaps he ought to go join him, explain it had all been a mistake. But the vision of a girl's tearful, imploring face presented itself to him from the depths of the pool and he knew that this way was impossible.

Sunk in meditation, he ceased to cast stones into the pool and, as the eddying waters settled into glass-like calm, so too his troubled thoughts seemed to resolve into tranquil clarity.

Once he'd stood at the mouth of the mighty Mississippi where it flowed into the sea and, some-how, he felt that the experience was akin to what was happening to him now. Salt water mixed with sweet, just as the bitter dissolution of his friendship with Jim was leavened by the tender feelings that were awak-ening in him for Rachel. And – like the river – there was no choice for him; he had to press on with the course that Fate had set him and take his chances in the great unknown before him.

That much settled in his mind, he flung a handful of the remaining pebbles into the water and climbed back on to his horse with the determined movement of a man who knows what he's doing and knows it's right, and headed back to the Anderson place.

Wade was not alone in the turbulence of his feelings over recent events. As he rode into town, Jim, too, was undergoing strong emotion about the way things had gone. But his sentiments were predominantly those of anger and a sense of betrayal. He reckoned his partner had ditched him for the charms of an attractive female. Not that he blamed the younger man for falling prey to womanly wiles, but to turn his back on an *amigo* on that account! Such a transgression was unforgivable in the code of the trail. Or so he figured anyway.

His mood of despondency was not lightened by the gruesome companion dogging his journey – the rapidly stiffening corpse of Bud Lewis. Every now and again Jim would twist in the saddle to check that the body had not slipped off its mount to tumble groundward. Or so he told himself. But at the back of his mind was the totally irrational fear that his fallen foe would spring to life and leap on him from behind to drag him along down to the Hell where he was most surely bound.

It was with some relief that he saw again the sprawl of wooden buildings and dusty streets that made up the town of Little Pine, the very place they had set out from the day before.

He made his way along the main street, his eyes searching for the sheriff's office, avoiding the gaze of the few town folk abroad at this time of day, who stared at him and his morbid cargo in open-mouthed astonishment.

When he had located the place he was looking for, he tethered the animals to a hitch rail and strode on in.

He found himself in a dark, grimy sort of room,

with faded wanted posters on the wall and a few pieces of crude furniture set around a floor that badly needed sweeping. The only decent accoutrement in this sorry excuse for an office was a fine, old-fashioned desk festooned with numerous drawers and ornate compartments but whose broad top was heavily scarred with what seemed like the rowels of countless boots. The place appeared deserted and, figuring that the sheriff might have stepped out for a while, Jim was about to go looking elsewhere, when a faint and unmusical sound reached him from out of the dim recesses. Straining his eyes into the gloom, he perceived that there was another door at the back with a small square opening fitted with iron bars. He advanced toward it as the strange whistling sound seemed to come from this direction. Once he got to the door he peered through the bars. This was obviously the prisoners' cell and slumped on a filthy palliasse was a crumpled figure, a whiskey bottle clutched in one hand and his hat slouched over his unshaven face. Evidently it was some drunken cowpoke sleeping it off from the previous night's revelries. Jim was about to withdraw from this embarrassing sight of a man wallowing in liquor-sodden degradation, when the sleeper gave another of his little snores and turned over to settle himself in a more comfortable position. In the fitful light that filtered through a narrow window, Jim caught the glint of metal on the man's chest and realized with a start that it was a lawman's badge. Shaking his head ruefully, he pushed on the cell door, which swung open with a protesting creak of its rusty hinges. He didn't expect much from the poor specimen who lay before him, but he had to report the killing to someone and – for better or worse – this was the only representative of law and order in these parts.

He bent down, pulling a face at the mixture of sweat and alcohol that assailed his nostrils and gave the recumbent figure a none-too-gentle shake.

'Eh . . . wha. . . ? Tarnation, can't a man get some shuteye around here?'

The sheriff tried to ignore the tugging on his arm and turned to the wall to settle back into the pleasant slumber he had been enjoying.

But Jim was insistent.

'Wake up, Sheriff, I gotta body outside that's gettin' a little ripe in the sun. I want you to take it off my hands.'

The lawman sat up grumpily, scratching his matted hair and looked at Jim peevishly then at the bottle still clutched in his hand. He examined it closely through half-shut, bloodshot eyes before tossing it away in disgust.

'Yah . . . empty,' he said irritably. Then he turned to Jim. 'Did you say you had a body outside, mister?'

'Yup,' said Jim, glad to see he'd finally got the old fellow's attention.

The sheriff struggled to his feet and pulled on a pair of scuffed boots. Then he jammed a battered Stetson on to his head and turned to Jim.

'Let's go see.'

When they emerged outside there was a small crowd gathered around the corpse. The sheriff stood for a few seconds, squinting to adjust his eyes to the sunlight before advancing to shoo away the curious onlookers.

'Step aside there, folks. I got the matter in hand. Just go about your business as normal.'

Despite the seediness of his appearance, the man still had some air of authority about him and the cowed citizens parted in front of him like the Red Sea before Moses. Now that he could see him better, Jim realized that the man was rather old to be toting a tin star. Given the general slovenliness of his person and the possible ageing effects of alcoholic over-indulgence, it was hard to say, but Jim would have put him on the shady side of sixty. He got the feeling from the calm and professional way that the fellow took death in his stride that he had held the office of lawman for quite a while. Maybe even had been a good one once. But those days seemed long gone.

The sheriff jerked up the head of the dead man with hard-eyed detachment.

'Hmmm . . .' was his only comment. Then he cast a weary glance at Jim. 'You'd best come with me, mister. You got some explainin' to do.'

Then he glanced with annoyance at the lingering band of citizens.

'Didn't I ask you to go about your business?' he demanded.

Reluctantly the knot of onlookers began to break up. But the oldster grabbed one by the arm as he was on the point of departing.

'Go get the undertaker, Tom, and tell him he's got a new client.'

Then he waved Jim into his office, pulled open a drawer on his desk and took out a half-full bottle of whiskey.

'Drink?' he offered Jim.

Jim shook his head, a look of distaste crossing his face. The sheriff noted his reaction but threw back the bottle nevertheless and took a long thirsty gulp of the amber fluid.

'A hair of the dog that bit me,' he said as he wiped his lips with relish and replaced the bottle in its resting place. Then, with a more business-like air, he produced a stubby pencil and tattered notebook, settled himself in a roundback chair and, leaning back, propped his spurred boots on top of the old desk, adding fresh score-marks to its much-scarred surface.

'OK, cowboy,' he said, giving the pencil lead a lick. 'Let's have it. Right from the start.'

CHAPTER 4

It didn't take Jim long to tell his story – which was a simple and straightforward one. The sheriff noted it all down in a laborious, scrawling hand, every now and again tossing in a terse, matter-of-fact question to clear up any minor detail that puzzled him. An onlooker would have taken the scene for an everyday transaction like a steer tally or a chore list being discussed by the two men instead of the account of mayhem and death, which was the real subject matter of their conversation.

Eventually the sheriff, who went by the name of Dooley, seemed satisfied and threw his notebook back into the drawer with a relieved sigh.

'Never was much of a one for writin',' he said, taking another pull on his bottle before stowing that away too.

Noticing the anxious look on the other man's face, he switched on a reassuring grin.

'Never mind about Bud,' he exclaimed cheerfully. 'He was a mean ol' polecat that had it comin'. Already killed two men I know of. He'd pick on some poor sodbuster, rile him into slappin' leather, then gun him down without battin' an eyelid. His kind won't be missed – 'cept by the undertaker.'

Taking this as a kind of dismissal, Jim lifted his hat and headed for the door.

Dooley coughed and called after him in an embarrassed tone.

'Just one thing, mister. Lewis had some hardcase friends that hang around town some. Might save us all a lot of trouble if you was to keep right on movin'.'

Jim stopped in his tracks without turning round. He sensed that Dooley was more concerned with his own safety than that of a drifting stranger. The man was obviously keen on the quiet life, marking time until his rapidly approaching retirement. Jim wasn't sure as he could blame him. But he wasn't about to let someone dictate to him whether he stayed or left. Especially as he was innocent of any crime.

'I'll think on it,' he replied, in a studied, neutral tone.

Somehow the way he said it did nothing to reassure the ageing lawman and, as the door of his shabby office slammed shut, Dooley's face bore a strained, weary look and unconsciously his hand strayed once more towards the drawer containing his recently abandoned whiskey bottle.

This Texan was trouble – he had been a lawman long enough to know that. But how or when the trouble would explode and who would be the ones to get hurt, this much worried him. As it happened, he wouldn't have long to find out.

Jim made his way directly to the saloon on quitting the sheriff's office. He was thirsty and tired after his long ride in and wanted to have a quiet drink and give some serious consideration to his next move. Besides it was always possible that his partner might have second thoughts and come after him; it was best he stick around some rather than get too far ahead on the trail.

He cast a casual glance around the room as he stepped into the shady and pleasingly cool interior. There weren't too many customers at this time of the day, just the usual collection of loafers and doleful-looking drunks already engaged in the daily task of drowning the sorrows of a wasted existence. Only one figure stood out from this nondescript crowd: a tall man seated on his own in a corner in front of a whiskey bottle from which he seemed to be partaking only sparingly. He wore good-quality, well-tailored clothes of a sombre hue but his lined, weathered face under a tan Stetson bore the stamp of a stockbreeder rather than a storekeeper. Jim caught the astute glint of sharp blue eyes as their gaze crossed briefly before he sauntered to the bar to order a beer.

He had taken a mere few sips of his drink and was just savouring its refreshing coolness, when the batwings swung open to admit two newcomers to the company. They were not a savoury sight. One was a

45

hulking giant of a man, his bulk consisting as much of beer-belly as brawn. His face bore the scarred and coarsened look of a street brawler and the pistol that dangled at his side seemed like a child's toy in comparison to immense, ham-like fists. He stood with his thumbs hooked in his belt, feet spread out, and surveyed the room with arrogant disdain, his piggy eyes roving challengingly for the least sign of defiance from anyone there.

Beside him was a complete contrast in physical appearance: a scrawny, half-starved-looking individual dressed almost in rags, with wild, staring eyes. From the toes of his scuffed, heel-worn boots to the brim of his filthy, well-ventilated hat, this gent had the look of a hobo on hard times. The only exception to this general air of negligence and grime in his attire was the sleekly gleaming gun-rig he wore, adorned on each side by the protruding ivory butts of two shining Colts.

He seemed to gloat in the physical menace of his companion, relishing the look of fear that had crept into many men's faces upon the dramatic entry of this sinister pair.

A lion and his jackal, thought Jim, as he gave them a long hard stare before turning his attention back to his glass. He had seen the combination before and it was a loathsome one. A dangerous one too, for it twinned the two evils of reckless violence with cold-blooded cunning. The gaze of the goliath raked the room and men's eyes dropped before its savage intensity. But at last his focus honed in on the one man he was seeking. He looked questioningly at his confederate who nodded hard-eyed.

'Reckon that's him, Bull. Let's go get 'im.'

The big man felt a surge of rising pleasure as he swaggered across the floor towards his intended victim, with his malign accomplice scurrying glee-fully behind him. He knew he was going to enjoy this. He always did. He'd start off slow, baiting the fellow a little, like poking at a captured animal. Then he'd get a little more insistent, push him further towards his limit, humiliate him openly with foul, filthy insults. If that didn't provoke the man into fighting, he'd throw a drink into his face or knock him to the floor. All the time he'd be sporting himself, like a cat playing with a mouse, revelling in the struggle of the victim's fear with his self-respect, as the pressure was relentlessly applied and the torture-rack of public degradation tightened notch after agonizing notch until something broke. And that something would be either the man's spirit or his temper. Either he turned and fled, never to be seen in town again, or else he exploded into furious fight. Bull liked it best when it came down to violence. He liked to feel the raw power he got as he beat his opponent to bloody, smashed submission. He'd never had any success with women, who turned in repulsion from his ugly, ungainly appearance, nor had he ever had much brains to impress others with his cleverness. His only gift was sheer brute force and he gloried in the ability this gave him to destroy the beauty and intelligence he envied.

'You, mister,' he said stopping beside Jim, with a sneer of malice on his lips, 'you're new in town.'

Jim turned languidly and favoured him with an indifferent glance.

'Yep.'

'Figgerin' on stickin' around?'

'Mebbe.'

The big man was getting irate at Jim's coolness of manner. He decided to speed things up a little.

'Don't say much, do you?' he jeered.

'Nope.'

A titter of amusement arose from the back of the otherwise deathly silent room and Bull turned to glower at the crowd. He was being made to look a fool by this laconic drifter and he didn't like it. It was time to cut short the usual build-up and bring things to a head.

'I hear you're siding with sod-busters, friend. That ain't healthy. I reckon you've outstayed your welcome in this town. Get your gear and ride.'

A glint of iron entered Jim's eyes as he surveyed his challenger.

'But I ain't finished my drink yet,' he said mildly.

Bull failed to notice the expression on Jim's face and put this objection down to obtuseness.

'Let me spell it out for you, dumbass. If you don't hightail it right now, I'm gonna bust you up so good your own ma wouldn't know you.'

He turned to give smirk of triumph to his disreputable associate. Now he'd laid it out plain for the slow witted son-of-a-bitch. But, as he swivelled his head back, a flying, rock-like object collided with his jaw and he staggered back a few feet, surprised by its sudden impact.

He shook himself to clear his spinning head and tried to gather his senses. Before him floated a vision of Jim, fists raised, head lowered and a look of grim resolution on his countenance. It was then that Bull understood what had occurred. The drifter had actually hit him. At the same time he tasted blood in his mouth and realized that the blow had done some damage, though nothing serious. Hot rage welled up in him, like an erupting volcano, and he charged mindlessly at the insolent stranger, fists swinging like battering rams. But he only connected with air, as his opponent sidestepped him and stuck out a foot which Bull obligingly sailed over to land with a resounding thud on the wooden planks of the floor.

Jim stood over his fallen adversary, fists clenched and eyes glowing with a dangerous fire. But all fight seemed to have been knocked from the winded Bull. He just lay there, quietly moaning and nursing his ugly head. This could have been Jim's chance to finish the fight there and then with a few well-aimed kicks into the ample gut of his fallen foe. Indeed, Bull appeared to be almost inviting this as he lay there like an oversized slug, his shirt pulled up to expose the obscene creases of his swollen belly. But it was not Jim's way to attack a man who lay defenceless on the ground. Besides, he had the sneaking suspicion that, with the craftiness of a seasoned brawler, Bull was mostly feigning his helplessness, trying to lure his opponent in for the kill before recovering with sudden energy and launching a vicious counter-attack.

So instead he stood off, catching his breath and watching Bull warily. The big man slowly started to heave himself up, using a table for support. Then, with a lightning burst of movement, he grabbed a bottle and flung it at the Texan. Jim was quick enough to avoid this missile but not the mass of flesh and bone that followed as Bull hurtled himself upon him. He was bowled over and knocked to the floor by the giant's massive weight and felt a sensation almost of drowning as the air was squeezed out of him by the fleshy bulk pressing down on him. Desperately he struggled to break free but he was well and truly trapped, malevolent eyes staring into his from a mere few inches away as he smelt the fetid odour of his enemy's foul breath in his nostrils.

'I got you now, boy,' Bull crowed triumphantly, 'and you're gonna hurt . . . hurt like you never done before. Yessirree, ol' Bull's gonna teach you a lesson you won't never forget.'

To reinforce the point he drove his fist hard twice or three times into the Texan's jaw. Jim slumped, semi-conscious and his tormentor hauled himself upright, resting either knee on his victim's spread-eagled arms. That left his hands free to work the man over at his leisure. He would concentrate on the face; once Bull had finished with him, no woman would ever look at the Texan again without a shudder of horror, or any man without a shiver of fear. With sadistic relish, he drew back his fist to deliver a blow that would shatter the man's nose to a bloody pulp.

But Bull had no monopoly on the game of playing possum. All the while Jim had been acting more stunned than he really was, closely watching his opponent through half-closed eyes. Now, while Bull was off-balance and poised to strike, Jim suddenly bucked like a powerful mule and the big man went flying over him, smacking the foot-rail of the bar on the side of his head with a metallic clang as hard bone collided with even harder brass.

In a trice, Jim was on his feet again, just as fit to carry on the fight as he'd ever been. But that wasn't the case with his burly protagonist. He just lay there moaning softly, all bravado knocked out of him and patently unable for further combat.

At that moment came a high-pitched giggle, like that of an hysterical woman, arrested suddenly by a yelp of surprise. Jim wheeled round to see Bull's ragged companion slowly raising his skinny hands from his gun-butts, his features a picture of thwarted wrath and fear. Behind him, with a Colt revolver jammed into the miscreant's back, stood the well-dressed rancher whom Jim had noticed earlier. But now his face was set in an expression of determined and deadly menace that transformed his whole appearance. Jim realized that this was the real man inside the fancy clothes and, judging from his demeanour, he was not a man to cross.

'Put your hands up – real slow, Scarecrow,' rasped the older man.

The aptly named scoundrel couldn't see who'd got the drop on him but he felt the business end of a pistol against his spine and the harsh-edged voice sounded like it belonged to someone who just might use it.

His hands ascended upwards while his eyes shifted nervously from side to side.

With expert deftness, the rancher extracted scarecrow's irons from his holsters and tossed them with a noisy clatter on the bar counter.

'You can collect them later. Meantime help up that no-account cousin of yours and drift.'

Scarecrow lowered his arms with alacrity and went to the aid of his outsized relative, casting only an apprehensive side glance at the stern issuer of these commands. Staggering under the smothering bulk of the semi-conscious Bull, he made for the street, pausing only at the doorway to turn and make the following threat.

'Folk think you're real big in these parts, Jackson, but maybe it was time you was cut down to size. Me and Bull—'

But he didn't get any further, for a shot rang out and yet another hole was formed in his already well-aired hat as it parted company with his greasy scalp. As though jerked by an invisible string, Scarecrow and Bull did a lightning vanishing act and the sound of rapidly retreating footsteps could be heard scurrying away down the sidewalk.

When Jackson turned to Jim, the look of grimness had disappeared from his face and was replaced by a look of almost boyish enjoyment.

'Wanted to do that for some time, mister. Thanks for giving me the excuse.'

Jim shook his head smilingly.

'It's me who ought to thank you. You just saved my life there. That coyote was fixin' to plug me for sure and would've done too if you hadn't played a hand.'

'Forget it, friend,' rejoined the other, setting his gun easily back into its holster. 'That was one hell of a whipping you just gave to that varmint Bull. Seeing that was repayment for any favour I done you.'

'Let me buy you a drink though,' persisted Jim, eager to show his gratitude.

'OK, but it's me that's buying the drink. Barman, get my special bottle and bring it to my table.'

When they'd sat down, Jackson opened the fresh bottle and poured Jim a shot, then knocked back his own with a flourish.

Jim followed suit. It was good stuff. Went down smooth as silk, then hit the belly like a mule kick. His host poured another.

'My name's Nathan Jackson. I ranch in these parts. Gotta spread called Zion. Maybe you've heard of it.'

Jim reached out to shake Jackson's proffered hand.

'Langford's my name, just call me Jim though. Can't say I've heard of your place. I'm new to this territory and only passing through.'

The rancher cast Jim an appraising look.

'Are you in the cowboyin' line yourself, Jim?'

'I done some,' said Jim guardedly. 'Though not in a while.'

'Then maybe you'd be interested in a job,' proposed Jackson, leaning forward slightly with a glint of keenness in his eyes.

Jim reflected a little, toying with his glass meditatively. That morning he'd been angry with his partner. Still was. But that didn't mean he'd run out on him over a few cross words. They went too far back for that. The habit of friendship and interdependence was too deeply ingrained by now. He'd stick around until the kid came to his senses. Meantime, a job wasn't such a bad idea.

'Mebbeso,' he said finally, knocking back another swallow of whiskey. 'Are you offerin'?'

'Reckon I am,' answered Jackson. 'I'm finding it kind of hard to get good hands right now. The sort who know how to use shootin' irons as well as brandin' irons. You look that sort to me. There's trouble breaking in this valley. Big trouble. I aim to protect what's mine, but I need some backin' up. You can help provide that.'

'I'll think on it,' said Jim non-committally. Actually

he had already made up his mind, but there was no reason in appearing *too* eager to a prospective employer. 'First off I'd like to see the set-up.'

Jackson beckoned to the barman.

'No time like the present. I'll bring you out to the Zion right now. Have a mosey around today and eat with me and the boys this evening. Leave tomorrow after breakfast if you don't cotton to it. No obligation.'

Jim nodded. He could see that Jackson was not one to waste time. Men like him didn't get where they were through dallying. Action followed as close on the heels of thought as a buggy to a horse. That very afternoon Jim found himself being introduced to the rest of the Zion crew. There were a dozen men there, most of whom had been coming back every year for the spring drive. They seemed a good mix of young and old, the frolicsome with the steady, and each knew the other as well as they knew every corner of the 300,000 acre range.

Jackson had assured his welcome from the start by his blunt introduction of the newcomer to the tough bunch of range riders.

'This here's Jim Langford,' he announced, in curt, no-nonsense terms, 'He's just given a hell of a lickin' to Bull Casey, so I wouldn't cross him any, if he decides to ride for us.'

The men eyed Langford with interest. They knew that their boss was not a man who was easily impressed, yet this cool-eyed stranger seemed to have already won his trust and liking. Since those were exactly the sentiments they felt for their employer, they accepted his judgement and straightaway treated Jim as one of their own, so that in no time at all he felt right at home – or as much as he could ever feel at home outside of Texas. So the decision to stay was not a hard one – but, he still wondered at the back of his mind, was it the right one? Only time would tell.

CHAPTER 5

Morgan King was not a patient man; he did not take kindly to waiting. When it was occasionally necessary, he found it almost impossible to keep still and had to occupy his energetic nature with some kind of action to match the jostling of his restless thoughts. Now was such a time and he paced the length of his richly furnished study with rapid strides, stopping every so often at the window to tug aside the curtain and peer out anxiously.

By any measure he was an impressive-looking figure, with a thick mantle of iron-grey hair, a broad forehead and gimlet, blue eyes. His build was robust but the muscles on his body were turning somewhat to flesh for want of sufficiently vigorous use. One's gaze was drawn automatically to his hands which never seemed to be at rest, one moment rubbing his chin in thought, the next playing nervously with the expensive diamond ring that adorned one finger. These were large, powerful, as if meant to grasp a blacksmith's hammer or a bargeman's pole, but their pale, soft and smooth appearance showed that they were employed in less virile pursuits.

All in all, the impression King gave was of a man endowed by nature for an honest, healthy, outdoor kind of life but whose greed and deviousness had perverted that raw physical energy into a blind alley of ledger-books and profit margins.

The rancher arrested his restless pacing to consult the face of a grandfather clock that stood by the door, the sonorous beat of its heavy pendulum the only sound to disturb the silence of the house. He compared its time with a silver pocket watch and shook his head with a grimace of annoyance. His visitors were long overdue, but he knew that their kind paid scant respect to the niceties of punctuality, reckoning the hour only by a guess from the position of the sun.

Finally, however, he heard the tread of footsteps outside on the veranda, one set light and springy, the other cumbrous and plodding. Even before the door opened, he had already divined the identity of his callers, for they were the very ones he was expecting.

He was standing in front of the fireplace, his hands clasped behind his back when his guests were led sheepishly into his presence by a disdainful manservant. It was none other than that sorry pair of villains, Bull and Scarecrow.

The latter had made some sort of half-hearted attempt to spruce up his disreputable person. His battered boots had been treated to a long needed coat of polish to coax a dull gleam from the grimy leather. While not actually clean, his ragged clothes had at least been dusted off with a horse-brush, which had left them looking – if not smelling – a little better. His wild hair had been slicked down with some handy axle-grease but the yellowish, unshaven features beneath, with broken nose and crooked teeth seemed little improved by this toilette. At that moment, he was respectfully clutching his crumpled headgear, looking for all the world like a cur about to receive a whipping from its master.

As regards Bull, he was, on the face of it, his usual swaggering self. His hat remained jammed firmly on his head, his thumbs were hitched in his gunbelt and he hadn't so much as changed the beer-stained buck-skin shirt he habitually wore. Without waiting for an invitation, he plumped himself into the nearest chair, produced a florid bandanna and mopped his sweating brow.

'Sure is a hot one,' he remarked conversationally.

'I don't remember asking you to take a seat,' King growled, a steely edge of menace to his voice.

Bull leapt up as if stung by an invisible wasp. Like it was possessed of a life of its own, his hand flew to his hat, removed it and pressed it to his ample belly as a tardy sign of deference to his host.

'Sorry, Mr King,' he stammered. 'No offence meant.'

King pinned him with his icy stare for few seconds, much like a bug-hunter examining a trapped insect, then acknowledged his apology with a mirthless movement of his lips that might have passed for a smile except for the accompanying coldness of the eyes.

'I called you here,' he said, his gaze slipping off into the unfathomable distance, 'so that you could explain how that raid on the Anderson place a few nights ago went so wrong. Not only did you fail to burn down the place but you managed to lose my best man in the process.'

Bull and Scarecrow cast an apprehensive glance at one another. It was the smaller man who replied; as usual he was the mouthpiece of the duo.

'It weren't our fault, Mr King,' he whined. 'They jumped us. We was lucky to save our own hides.'

'Who jumped you?' cut in the rancher sarcastically. 'A young girl and her kid brother?'

'No, sir!' replied Scarecrow with alacrity. 'They had help. Professional gunmen just a-lyin' in wait.'

'Oh, yes,' continued King, feigning surprise. 'And how many of these desperadoes were there?'

For a fleeting second Scarecrow considered inflating the figure of the defending force but then he thought the better of it. King always seemed remarkably well-informed and hated being lied to.

'Well, ah, as a matter of fact . . . just two,' he admitted lamely, then added hastily, 'but they were Texans!'

King smiled ironically at this unconscious tribute to the prowess of the Lone Star State's fighting men.

'And where are these terrible Texans now?' he continued playfully.

'Well, thar's the thing. Seems they've had some sort of bust-up. One's still at the Andersons', t'other showed up in town the other day. Me and Bull braced him good and woulda laid him out cold but for Jackson steppin' in. Now we hear he's gone to work for him on the Zion range.'

'Jackson?' said King in a sudden spurt of anger. 'He'll rue the day he ever stuck his nose into my business. But for now he'll have to wait his turn while I deal with this latest pair of troublemakers.'

From the daily reports he received from the sheriff, King actually knew all about Jim and Wade and he had summoned the disreputable couple in front of him for another, entirely sinister purpose of his own. So he let the subject drop and an uncomfortable silence gradually seeped into the room as the cattleman appeared to lapse into his own thoughts.

'Well, ah,' muttered Scarecrow at last, 'if that's all, I guess we'll be getting back to our own business.'

'Business?' snapped King, returning to himself. 'You have no business except to do what I tell you, when I tell you. Is that understood?'

'Sure Mr King!' yelped the pair in unison.

'Good,' remarked the rancher. He pursed his lips and eyed the men narrowly as he proceeded with his palaver. 'Against my better judgement, I'm going to give you another chance. We're gonna get rid of the Andersons and that Texan who's helping them in

61

one clean sweep.'

Bull and Scarecrow exchanged alarmed glances. After recent experiences, they were not too keen to tangle with any Texans again in a hurry. King caught the look and read their fear.

'Don't worry,' he said, 'I'm not sending you on an ambush at the homestead after what happened last time. We'll find a way to trick Prescott into town. After that, the woman and the kid will be on their own . . . defenceless.'

The way he dwelt on the final word sent the imagination of the two scoundrels racing in such a way that they didn't even pause to consider how their boss, despite his earlier pretended ignorance, already knew Wade's name.

'What do you want us to do with 'em?' queried Bull eagerly.

'Anything you've a mind to,' countered King, his face as hard as flint. 'I'm through playing around. But don't kill them. Just use your powers of persuasion to make them up stakes and skedaddle. You can do that, can't you?'

Bull and Scarecrow nodded silently, an evil expression of devilish glee written on their unsavoury features. They would enjoy persuading the woman – enjoy it a lot. As for the kid, he'd be taken care of too. When Bull and Scarecrow were done with them, the Andersons would be only too glad to pack up and go.

Suddenly an unpleasant thought struck the skinny one.

'What'll Prescott do when he finds out?'

'Why he'll come gunnin' for you, of course,' rejoined King. 'But you'll be waiting for him; at a time and place of your own choosing and with plenty of firepower to back you up.'

Scarecrow looked somewhat reassured but still uneasy.

'But what if he joins up with that pardner of his – the one who's working for Jackson now?'

King was beginning to get annoyed.

'What if? What if? I give you a sure-fire plan and all you can give me back is a load of belly-achin'. Even with two Texans, you'll still have at least a dozen men on your side. That the kind of odds you can live with?'

The diabolical grin stole back on to Scarecrow's face as, reassured on this point, his thoughts turned back to the enticing vision of a beautiful, fresh young woman at his tender mercy.

'OK,' he nodded emphatically. 'We'll do it. But how are we gonna winkle Prescott out of there in the first place?'

'Leave that to me,' said King confidently. 'Just worry about *your* side and get the job done right this time.'

The malevolent expression on Scarecrow's countenance deepened even further.

'Don't you worry none about that, boss. We'll do it right. And it'll be a pleasure, a real pleasure.'

*

Wade was working on the roof of the damaged barn at the Anderson place when Sheriff Dooley rode in. The corpulent lawman looked sticky and uncomfortable from his long journey and seemed relieved to ease himself from the saddle of his mount. He led the animal to the water trough and doused his own head under the pump before eventually addressing Wade while wiping off his face.

'You must be Prescott. Mister King would like to see you. He's waiting in town right now.'

'Oh yeah?' said Wade, driving another nail home with a few unerring strokes. 'What's he want with me?'

'Just a friendly chat,' replied Dooley, setting his hat back on his head. 'It could be worth your while. King's a mighty powerful man in these parts.'

'Maybe I ain't in a conversational mood,' remarked Wade.

'If you're smart, you'll come and right away,' growled Dooley, suddenly annoyed. 'Mister King don't like waiting around.'

'How come he sent you anyways?' asked Wade, changing tack abruptly. 'You his message-boy or something?'

'No I ain't!' thundered the sheriff, now thoroughly beside himself. 'But it's my job to keep the peace around here. Maybe if you was as ready to talk as you are to fight, we might get somewhere.'

'I'm all for that,' countered Wade. 'But it ain't up to me. Rachel and Seth own this place. They're the ones King ought to be parleyin' with.'

'He's through tryin' to persuade those mule-headed nesters. Now he wants to see you and that pardner of yours. Reckons you could be a go-between in this whole sorry business.'

'Jim's still here?' asked Wade, astonished.

'Sure he is,' snapped Dooley. 'Got himself a job cowboyin' for a local rancher name of Nathan Jackson. King's sent one of his men to fetch him in, too.'

Wade was silent for a moment, considering the offer. He didn't like the idea of leaving Seth and Rachel on their own, but perhaps this was a genuine attempt to settle the conflict without further blood-shed. Things just couldn't go on the way they were. Besides, it would give him a chance to patch up the quarrel with his friend – a chance he feared he might never have again.

'OK,' he said finally. 'Rachel and Seth are off visit-ing a neighbour. When they get back, I'll talk this over with them. If they've got no objections, I'll be along to see King this afternoon. But this had better be no trick or. . . .'

The sheriff looked affronted.

'I wouldn't be party to any double-dealin' of that kind, mister. King told me that he's keen to settle this dispute and reckons you're his best chance to do it. Don't disappoint him.'

With that, he mounted his horse, turned its head with a tug of the reins and jabbed his spurs into the creature's haunches, departing in a flurry of dust.

Wade gazed after him thoughtfully. The man seemed genuine enough and the chance to bring peace to the valley, not to mention mending fences with his former partner, was too good an opportunity to miss. Why was it then that, beneath the thinking, logical side of him, there lurked the age-old animal instinct that scented danger and the trap and bade him – above all – to beware?

Wade's feeling of unease did not diminish on the trail into town. Indeed, if anything, it increased. He kept scanning the hills and plains around him for sign of a concealed ambush but, though none materialized, he felt at times as if he was being watched by unseen eyes and his vigilance did not relax for an instant nor did his hand stray very far from his six-shooter.

Rachel had not openly opposed his leaving the farm, yet it was clear from her manner that she was far from happy about it. But, for her part, she knew it would be folly to stand in the way of a reunion of the two friends and, even if nothing else came of the meeting with King, there was always hope of a reconciliation between the Texan trail-buddies. Wade had enjoined her and Seth to keep a close watch for trouble and not to stray too far from the house.

When he got to town, he reined his horse to the hitchrail and stepped up on to the sidewalk. There were two saloons in town, one for the more respectable townsfolk and the other – simply named Kate's Place after some previous owner – for less civilized types such as drovers. King had arranged to meet in a room at the former, which also served as a hotel. On his way to this rendezvous, Wade noticed several ponies with a distinctive rising sun brand tied up at Kate's. It was evident that King had brought an entourage of his Red Sun riders along for security. Wade felt relieved at this sight, for it meant that these men at least would not be involved in a sneak raid on the Andersons during his absence.

When he entered the bar, he spotted a familiar figure leaning against the counter. The man straightened up as he approached and they regarded each with an air of uncertainty. It was the younger man who broke the silence.

'Hello, Jim.'

' 'Lo, Wade.'

'Thought you'd moved on?'

'Nope, got offered a job and decided to stick around a spell.'

There was an awkward pause.

'Know what King wants with us?' asked Wade.

'Not a clue. I was waitin' on you before goin' up. Figured you might know.'

'One way to find out, I guess.'

'Only way.'

Both men checked their guns in unconscious imitation of each other, then dropped them back into their holsters. An onlooker would have no doubt that this was a ritual long practised by the pair and carried out without even thinking about it.

'Let's go.'

They mounted the stairs and stopped outside a door. One took up a position at the side, gun in hand, while the other knocked.

'Come in.' The response sounded relaxed and unthreatening.

Wade warily opened the door and surveyed the room. It contained only King, seated behind a heavy wooden table, a tumbler of whiskey in his hand and an amused smile on his face.

'You can tell your friend to holster up, too. This ain't no ambush.'

The two Texans entered the room, still cautious, their eyes searching for signs of danger. When they were satisfied there wasn't any, they turned their attention to the man who had, by dint of chance, become their mortal enemy. For a few seconds they regarded one another warily, as powerful animals might if they met suddenly in a forest clearing. Then King stood up and leant over the table to extend a hearty, welcoming hand.

'Glad to meet you boys. I've heard a heap about you. Set yourselves down and let me pour you a drink.'

A little overwhelmed at this enthusiastic greeting, the partners settled themselves into the proffered seats, all the while looking around suspiciously.

King noted their apprehension and roared with laughter.

'Aw, don't worry so! You act like you expect the ceiling to cave in on youse. This is just a friendly business chat, that's all.'

The duo relaxed a fraction. It seemed unlikely that King would risk his own hide with gunplay in such a confined space. Whilst they were with him, they were at least safe.

King poured two generous measures of whiskey for his guests and topped up his own glass again. After sipping on his drink, he surveyed the Texans shrewdly.

'I'll come straight to the point, boys. I figure you for cowboys, used to cattle and the open range. How come you're siding with the earth-grubbin' kind in this valley?'

It was Wade who replied.

'I ain't siding with anybody, Mr King. I just don't like to see innocent folk get run off their land by bully-boy tactics.'

King directed his glance at Jim.

'What about you? Feel the same way?'

Jim seemed uncomfortable with the question and shifted uneasily in his chair.

'I'm a cattleman through and through all right,' he said finally, 'and I don't hold with nesters. If you was to offer the Andersons a fair price for that land. . . .'

'Dang it!' King exploded. 'I could offer those dirt-farmers ten times the price and they still wouldn't shift. I know their sort – if they get their paws on a

69

piece of land, they just won't give it up until they're buried in it.'

'A man's gotta defend what's his,' countered Wade. 'Otherwise he ain't worth anything.'

With an effort, King controlled his rising irritation and switched smoothly to another approach.

'Look here, you men are drovers at heart. And you know how to handle trouble. Why not work for me? I'll pay top wages and a share of the profits. Hell, in a few years you might even be able to buy a place of your own.'

The two men looked at each other. They'd known one another for a long time and there was no need even to discuss the matter. Each knew exactly what the other was thinking.

'Sorry, King,' answered Wade. 'We don't cotton to your way of doing business. Terrorizing women and kids just ain't our style. Never has been, never will be.'

King bit hard on his lip. He wasn't used to such blunt talking, yet hadn't the brass neck to deny the charge against him.

'All right,' he finally managed to spit out. 'Go your own way and see where it gets you. But if you keep interfering where it don't concern you, just watch out. Anyone who gets in my path will be stomped on hard. And that's a promise!'

Taking this thinly veiled threat as a dismissal, Wade and Jim rose to their feet, thrust on their hats and saw themselves out, leaving King fuming over his whiskey.

Wade wore a thoughtful expression as they emerged on to the street. Jim knew the look and threw a questioning glance.

'What's eatin' you, *amigo*?'

'I don't know, Jim. Somethin' don't smell right. King put on a good show in there but I felt he was stallin' us, not really interested in buying us off.'

'Seemed genuine enough to me,' countered Jim, taking out a plug of tobacco and starting to roll a quirly. 'Sure was for real riled when we left him.'

'Maybe,' said Wade doubtfully. 'But I got the idea he was holdin' out on us, like he knew something that we—'

Just then his musings were interrupted by a flurry of hoof-beats as two riders galloped into town. The horsemen dismounted at Kate's Place, tied up their broncs alongside the others and swaggered into the saloon, noisily hooting and slapping each other on the back. The sight made Wade even more uneasy. It was as if the pair had just done something shameful and were covering up their guilt with sham bravado.

'You know those jaspers?' he asked, turning to his companion.

'Sorry to say, I do,' replied Jim. He went on to recount to Wade his recent run-in with the disreputable duo.

Wade listened with growing alarm.

'Sounds to me like they're in cahoots with King. What if this meeting was a set-up to draw me away from the farm? Maybe that's where those varmints have just come from, maybe. . . .'

He never got to finish the sentence as the whole diabolical ploy suddenly appeared to him with blinding clarity. Without another word, he stalked off towards his horse. He had to go back to the Anderson place — and fast — to see if the sickening premonition of terrible evil he felt was true. There wasn't another second to lose.

After a momentary hesitation, Jim tossed aside his unsmoked cigarette in disgust and followed in Wade's footsteps. He felt he was getting sucked into a situation that could have deadly consequences for one or both of them. But, given his character, he had no other choice. When it came down to it, a man had to back up his partner; it was as simple as that. That was the one star that guided him through the darkness of troubled times. Without it, there would be nothing but total blackness.

CHAPTER 6

The two men rode hard across the grassy plain, sparing neither themselves nor their horses in their haste. Only when the farm buildings were in sight did they slow down to a canter for fear of alarming the inhabitants, in the event that they were wrong and nothing untoward had happened.

But all seemed ominously quiet as they entered the yard. Only a creaking barn door broke the eerie silence that reigned in the place.

Wade dismounted, warily looking around him with vigilant eyes. He could see little outwardly amiss but the very fact that no one had come out to greet them or even check who they were was not a good sign. He tied up the reins of his sweating animal and was about to enter the house when he heard a low moan from the direction of the barn. As he approached it, a figure staggered out, his face pale, hair matted with blood.

'Seth!' he gasped. 'What's happened here?'

The boy made no reply, just lurched forward a few

paces and collapsed.

The two men dragged him over to the water trough where Jim took the bandanna he was wearing from round his neck, soaked it and mopped off the youngster's features. Once he was cleaned up a bit, Seth didn't look quite so bad and it turned out most of the blood had issued from a four-inch gash on the side of his head. Apart from that, he was only suffering from minor cuts and bruises and a bad case of concussion.

'What happened here?' repeated Jim, when the boy had come to himself under the surprisingly gentle ministrations of the trail-hardened drover.

'I dunno,' replied the youngster vaguely. 'I heard a noise in the barn and went to investigate when someone snuck up behind me and fetched me a good one. Don't rightly remember much after that until you gents arrived.' A sudden thought struck him. 'Is sis OK?'

The answer to this was provided by the return of a grim-faced Wade. While his partner had been tending Seth, the other Texan had darted into the house to see if Rachel had been harmed in any way. Jim could see from his demeanour that something awful had happened. For a long time Wade stared at the ground, fists clenched, eyes burning. Fearing the worst, Jim grabbed his speechless partner and hustled him to one side. If it was bad news, he didn't want the wounded Seth to hear it just yet

'Rachel's inside,' Wade at last broke the tense

silence. 'She's not bad hurt, far as I can see but they
. . . they. . . .' His voice trailed off in a choking sob as
the man gave in to the pressure of the emotion he
was feeling. In an instant his partner was by his side,
hand on shoulder, his face grave with concern and
sympathy.

'All right, *compadre*,' he said softly, 'All right. Main
thing is, she's still alive. Anything else can be healed
with a bit of time and care. Don't you go off the deep
end, 'cause she's gonna need you now more than
ever.'

With a visible effort, Wade pulled himself together.
He shook himself and wiped off the palms of his
hands, as if he were trying to cleanse himself of the
evil memory of what he's just seen.

'You're right, Jim,' he said in a tone of forced
control. 'Things need doing and I gotta keep a clear
head.'

Jim looked at him intently, with his hand still on
his shoulder. It was evident that his friend was under
great stress, but he was getting a grip of his emotions
now and better able to handle the situation.

'OK,' he said authoritatively, 'where's the nearest
neighbour?'

'The O'Farrells,' answered Wade dully. 'Up the
valley apiece. It's only about a half-hour ride there
and back.'

'Well,' said Jim, 'why don't you ride on out there
pronto and get Mrs O'Farrell to come here? Then
we'll take off into town to see if we can't find the doc.

Meantime, I'll look after the kid and the girl.'

Wade nodded agreement to this plan. It made sense. It was best that Rachel saw another woman at this time. There were things she might want to talk about that it would be easier to confide in another member of her sex rather than a male listener, no matter how sympathetic he might be.

Besides, it gave him something definite to do, something to blot out the sense of helplessness and despair he felt at the sudden, shocking twist of events – not to mention the growing tide of rage he felt within him, which threatened to overwhelm him with its savage bitterness.

Whilst he was gone, Jim put Seth to bed after reassuring him as to Rachel's overall well-being, without revealing to him precisely what had happened to her. He managed to deflect the boy's anxious enquiries with the assertion that his sister needed rest after her ordeal. Luckily Seth was in no condition to argue and meekly allowed himself to be bandaged up and put beneath blankets where he immediately fell into a deep sleep, as his body reacted to the physical trauma of the brutal attack on it.

As regards Rachel, he briefly looked in on her and was shocked by the appearance of this normally proud and self-possessed young woman. She was lying on a divan, covered by a spread, her face pallid and bruised, red-rimmed eyes staring straight at the ceiling. She didn't even break her steadfast gaze on Jim's entry; from experience he recognized the classic signs of shock and withdrew tactfully. His fussing and fretting wouldn't help matters any.

Presently Wade returned with a ruddy-complexioned, middle-aged woman who bestrode a horse with an elegant ease that belied her stout build. She immediately dismounted, entered the house and within a short space of time had taken over things so comprehensively that the two men found themselves out on the veranda and idle for the first time since their arrival.

Their next most pressing task was to ride into town and fetch the doctor. But, besides this, there was another urgent matter to attend to.

'You know who did this?' It was Jim who posed this terse question.

'Yeah, it was those two we saw rein up at the saloon – the big, ugly one and the skinny, mean one.'

'Bull and Scarecrow – like I figured. What do you aim to do about it?'

'What do you think?'

'They'll be waitin' on you.'

'Then I wouldn't want to disappoint them.'

There was a pause and the two looked away.

'I'm in on it, too.'

'You don't have to be.'

'I said, I'm in on it,' Jim cut in, flat and hard. Wade didn't argue. He knew his friend was not to be dissuaded. Besides, he would need all the help he could get. He realized that he was walking into an elaborate trap but he couldn't see any way out of it.

If he turned his back on this monstrous crime and rode away, he might live to a ripe old age, but, as far as he was concerned, he would merely be a walking dead man. Every fibre of him rebelled at the very thought of it. No – better to die in the defence of justice and decency than live in a coward's world of callous selfishness.

'All right,' he said shortly. 'Let's go.'

The nearer they got to town, the more the mood of the two men changed. The shock and horror of what had happened at the Anderson place was wearing off and was replaced by a new, more dangerous passion – the thirst for vengeance. Perversely, this was almost a relief to the pair; in the hard life of a cowboy, more tender emotions like pity and sympathy were almost a hindrance and a nuisance. Living cheek by jowl with Nature, with its quota of prairie-fires, flash floods and droughts, death never seemed very far away. In the huge expanse of the grasslands, human life itself appeared tiny and precarious indeed, at the mercy of all sorts of mischance, both natural and man-made. Sentimentality and softness were out of place in this harsh environment; toughness and sheer grit were the qualities that kept a man alive.

So, without realizing it, Jim and Wade slipped into a groove with which they were well familiar, one which they had often known before. Their task seemed simple to them, without any troublesome emotional overtones to obscure their sole mission: to kill or be killed.

Thus the two men who entered Sheriff Dooley's office that afternoon were substantially different from the two who had set out from the Anderson holding a few hours before. This pair seemed sure of themselves, set on a course of action, determined and implacable. They had already located the town's doctor and dispatched him to Rachel's aid; now there remained one more chore to attend to.

The lawman gave a start when he saw them and uneasily put down the cup of coffee he was drinking. For once he was favouring this beverage over his favourite tipple, sensing somehow at the back of his mind that this day of all days was one when he'd need to keep his wits about him.

He surveyed his visitors, a quizzical look on his face.

'How can I help you, gents?'

Wade exchanged a glance with Jim. For a man at the heart of a fiendish plot, Dooley's manner was remarkably relaxed and cool.

'You know why we're here, Dooley,' declared Jim.

'Nope,' replied the sheriff with blunt sincerity. 'Not a clue. Maybe you can enlighten me?'

Wade looked at him hard. The man appeared genuinely in the dark about what had happened, despite the fact that it was he who had delivered the message that had lured him away from the farm. Dooley wasn't off the suspicious list yet but he sure as hell acted as if he was innocent. The Texan decided to play it cagey and observe the man's reactions carefully, watching to catch him in a lie.

'We're here to report a crime,' he said.

'Oh yeah?' countered Dooley blandly, reaching down to produce his tattered notebook from the recesses of its drawer. 'Let's have the details.'

As the cowboys related the course of that morning's events, the constable scribbled away furiously, but as they got towards the end of their narrative, his pen got less and less busy and an expression of black thunder slowly entered the old man's grizzled features. Eventually he stopped writing altogether.

'By God!' he exclaimed. 'Do you think I was part and parcel of this? Sure, King asked me to ride out and invite you in, but I thought it was a real attempt at a peace parley, not some kind of trick. He took me in the same way as he did you, that's the honest truth, fellows. It's a fact I ain't the lawman I once was. Maybe I'm a bit too partial to a bottle of liquor and maybe I turn a blind eye to some things it's healthier for me not to see, but you don't honestly think that I've sunk that low yet?'

The Texans regarded one another. Dooley was probably just a gullible dupe in this whole affair – that much seemed obvious now. The real villains were celebrating their infamy in a bar just a stone's throw from where they stood. Behind them, lurked an even more sinister and malevolent presence, further removed from the dirty work, but every bit as

culpable – indeed more so, since his cold and calculating brain had inspired the excesses of his corrupt
underlings. But the chief malefactor would have to
wait for his comeuppance. The simple fact of the
matter was that his hirelings were there, while he
wasn't. They had been named, the evidence against
his involvement had still to be found. What Jim and
Wade had to do now was plain, the rest they could
figure out later.

They turned as one to head for the door when
Dooley interjected.

'I gotta a favour to ask of you boys. I've an idea
where you're goin'; let me come with you. We'll give
them varmints a chance to surrender themselves for
trial. And if they don't . . . well, then justice will have
to be handed out there and then. At least that way,
nobody can say it wasn't done fair and legal.'

Jim chewed on this for a second or two. There was
a point in what the old buzzard had said. If they had
a peace officer with them, even in the rather washed-
out and sorry form of the present incumbent, it
might save any complications with the authorities
afterwards. There was a danger, of course, that this
was yet another trick, that Dooley would side with
their opponents in the showdown that would almost
certainly result and add to their already no doubt
considerable firepower. But a scrutiny of Dooley's
earnest, almost pleading expression convinced him
of the man's sincerity. Whether the ageing and
whiskey-sodden constable would be of any use in a

shoot-out was a moot point but here was a man seeking redemption and it was not his place to refuse him that second chance.

He turned to Wade for confirmation of this decision but he knew that his younger partner had been through the same thought processes and likely reached the same conclusion. A terse nod confirmed this assumption.

'OK, Dooley,' he said, 'you're in. But remember, if there's any funny business, you make an awful big target. And that tin badge just ain't big enough to stop a bullet.'

Dooley looked pathetically grateful and, throwing open another drawer of his old escritoire, pulled out a battered but formidable-looking sawn-off shotgun.

'Meet my partner, fellows,' he said, running his hand lovingly over the stock. 'He don't say much but when he does, by God, everybody listens.'

Despite the grimness of their mood, the Texans couldn't help smiling at the almost boyish enthusiasm with which the oldster was going to war. Perhaps it wasn't such a bad idea to have him along after all. Certainly the scattergun added considerably to their artillery and its owner had the air of one ready to use it.

Perhaps it wasn't surprising then that it was Dooley who, after checking his weapon and shoving a handful of fresh cartridges into his pocket, made the next move by announcing with an air of grim determination, 'It's time to pick up some bad men. Either dead or alive.'

And the way he said the latter showed he didn't much care which one it was.

CHAPTER 7

Things were pretty lively at Kate's Place around this time. The saloon was packed with King's men and the whiskey was flowing freely in the noisy, smoky atmosphere. Warmed by liquor and the glow of camaraderie, Scarecrow and Bull were bragging about recent feats and the things they intended to do in the near future. The imminent demise of certain meddling Texans figured largely in those plans. King wasn't there himself but he'd paid his minions well for their services and it was this gold that was being used to feed the not inconsiderable thirst of the assembled rannies.

There must have been about a score of men in the room, all tough range-riders and packing a fair amount of shooting ironmongery between them. Anyone would have supposed that two men against such a crowd would have no chance – would get gunned down in a second without even clearing leather. But a keener observer of human nature might have noted just a few things that didn't sit right with the air of impregnability that seemed to surround the company. He might have detected just an element of nervous tension in the constant joking and guffawing in the circle around Bull and Scarecrow; might have speculated on the reason for the occasional quick, furtive glances at the batwing doors that led on to the street; might have asked himself why men drinking such large quantities of alcohol should be licking on dry lips. The answer to this mystery would soon become apparent when the doorway darkened with the shape of two tall figures as, side by side, Jim Langford and Wade Prescott stepped into the bar.

Immediately the atmosphere of the place changed dramatically. The warm, heady ambience of whiskey fumes and cheerful human company drained away as from a sieve and was replaced by an icy, almost liquid silence that seemed to drench the very air. Some men even felt themselves ashiver; all were suddenly stone cold sober. Many of those present were puzzled by this abrupt shift of mood; others recognized it from before and knew that it meant only one thing – that Death had just appeared in the room and would not leave until it had exacted its tribute of blood.

No word was uttered but none was needed. The only sound was the scraping of chairs as those nearest Bull and Scarecrow tried to edge away discreetly. They figured that when the lead started flying, it would not be a good idea to be in their vicinity.

As regards those two ruffians, they seemed

momentarily frozen in the position where chance had found them, one holding a hand of cards, the other about to stub out his cigar. It was as if they dared not move, dared not even breathe for fear of bringing a hail of destruction upon their ugly heads. In their blanched faces only their eyes appeared alive, glistening with terror as they anxiously surveyed their grim-visaged foes.

And the Texans were certainly a sight to strike dread into the bravest of hearts. Both had entered with a six-gun grasped in each hand, the knuckle-bones showing white upon the triggers and a look of implacable resolution stamped sternly on their features. It was obvious to everyone that these were men of very determined and deadly purpose and to cross them would be to court the utmost peril. Against such adversaries the advantage of superior numbers suddenly seemed to dwindle drastically. Men were now watching Scarecrow and Bull to see what their play would be. It all depended on them.

Scarecrow came to himself first, looking around at his cohorts as if to remind himself of the overwhelming strength of his side.

'You gents gotta beef?' he jeered disdainfully. 'Me and Bull are ready to settle it with you in a fair fight. You shoot us now, there's a roomful of witnesses who'll testify you gunned us down in cold blood. That's a hangin' matter. Assumin' you stay alive that long.'

As he said the words, his own confidence grew.

Sure he'd been spooked by the dramatic arrival of the Texans, but that was what Mr King had counted on. The trap had worked and the victims had walked straight into it. Now was the time to spring it shut.

But then a voice spoke out from behind. A voice oddly familiar, yet with a new note of steely force to it.

'All right, *amigos*, just ease your mitts off those gun butts, loosen your rigs and drop your weapons to the floor. All 'cept Bull and Scarecrow. Like the man said, there's a beef to settle and I'm here to see it's done fair and square.'

All heads twisted incredulously to behold Sheriff Dooley standing on a small balcony that overlooked the whole scene. Somehow the man had spirited himself up the backstairs and now commanded the high ground in a bold stratagem that dramatically transformed the entire situation.

For a second the men looked at each other. But it took no genius to figure out that they'd been thoroughly outsmarted. With four guns pointed towards them from the front and the sheriff covering the rear with what appeared to be a small cannon, the chances of getting seriously hurt or worse had suddenly shot up. There was a ragged clatter as, one by one, the Red Sun crew dropped their firearms to the ground. Only Bull and Scarecrow, exempt from the order, seemed petrified into inaction; they were still frozen in their original stance like grotesque dummies in a show of horrors, all the more so since their faces turned an even waxier shade of white.

The floor gradually cleared until only the two miscreants remained there, marooned by their cowardly comrades.

The wily Scarecrow tried one last desperate ploy.

'You can't stand for this, Sheriff. If there's a charge against us, you oughta arrest us. There's gotta be a trial, a judge, witnesses.'

'Well, son,' countered Dooley, 'I reckon on this occasion, I'll save the county some money on all that legal carry-on. 'Sides, it was your suggestion to decide it here and now, man to man. This is your big moment, I'll see you get a fair shake.'

Bull and Scarecrow exchanged glances. Maybe the lawman was right – at least this way they had a chance. If they plugged the Texans in a fair fight, the old-timer could do nothing about it; in fact would be alone then at the mercy of the mob. There was only one way out and they had to take it.

Scarecrow, as usual, spoke for the two of them.

'OK,' he said, in a shaky voice he hardly recognized as his own. 'A straight gunfight. But them varmints have to holster up first. It's gotta be from the draw, that's the only square way.'

Without a word the Texans stowed away their pistols, one in the holster and one tucked through the belt buckle. Bull and Scarecrow relaxed somewhat now that there were no longer four guns trained on them. At this point they figured they were on level ground – more than level – for they both fancied themselves quick-draw shootists of no mean skill. Only there was still that little, niggling doubt; the two men opposite seemed so calm, so composed, as if they'd been in this situation before too. The two cousins spread out and took up the familiar gunman's half-crouch, hands hovering over their weapons, every nerve strained towards that vital second which would spell salvation or destruction. Their antagonists, in contrast, did not budge an inch, just stood there stock-still, watching, waiting, poised.

Somehow something didn't sit right with Scarecrow. He just couldn't put his finger on it but there was something about the men that reminded him of an unpleasant memory – a warning. He put off the moment of reckoning as long as he could, part of his mind searching for the answer to the puzzle that dogged him. Out of the corner of his eye he caught a glimpse of Bull looking at him with a querying, urgent expression; as usual the big man was waiting for his crafty partner to make the decisive move, even in this mortal moment.

The hell with it, he finally thought. I'll figure it out later.

His hand flew towards his gun and was closing on the coldness of its butt when the room exploded, then seemed to plunge into utter darkness. Through the shadow he perceived a small light that grew rapidly until it became a picture of young boy staring at something in horrified paralysis, something hidden in the grass. As the vision brightened, he saw the object of the boy's terror: it was a deadly rattlesnake with its head raised up high in the striking pose, its beady eyes transfixing its victim with hypnotic malevolence, watching, waiting, poised. Now he knew what memory the sight of his enemies had stirred in him. And he realized that, though the snake had missed him on that day so long ago, it had finally struck his black heart in a vindictive leap down all the intervening years. He tried to utter some word of protest, some curse at the unfairness of it all, but his strength had fled him and, as the morbid image slipped away, so too were the last flickers of his consciousness extinguished and the shades of everlasting night prevailed.

A fraction slower than his kinsman, Bull's hand had not even touched his weapon when an ounce of hot lead drilled his ungainly head. His face still bore a look of snarling menace tempered with just the beginning of hopeless realization as he crumpled soundlessly to the floor.

For a moment all was still in the room, as in a chapel or a morgue. Only the acrid reek of cordite and the two bodies sprawled across each other on the floor, inseparable in death as in life, gave any sign of the terrible drama that had just occurred.

The two Texans still stood there, rock-steady and hard-eyed, guns gripped level and ready for the slightest sign of provocation to renew their savage onslaught. But action against this deadly duo was the last thing on the minds of King's men. They merely gaped in horror from the blood-spattered, tangled heap of corpses to the menacing muzzles of their grim-faced slayers. It was enough to daunt the bravest of men and the cowardly jackals who served Morgan King had no stomach for a helping of the treatment lately meted out to their dead *compadres*.

Seeing no threatening movement on the part of their adversaries, the pair started to edge backwards towards the exit, their eyes and pistols never wavering from the men across the room. These, for their part, retained a frozen, sullen silence, fearful lest a sudden move might bring forth a withering crescendo of flying bullets. Only when the Texans had disappeared through the batwing doors did the company slowly return to life. Cautiously men cast a glance to the balcony where the forbidding figure of the sheriff had presided. But he, too, had mysteriously melted away. Reassured on this point, the bolder of them sprang forward to examine the bodies of their defunct comrades. Amidst an excited babble they frantically sought for indications of any lingering signs of vitality and, only incidently, to ascertain if the still-warm cadavers might have a few dollars about their persons. On both accounts they were to be sorely disappointed.

Unknown to all the participants in these events, there had been an interested spectator observing their every move from afar. Morgan King's room at the hotel commanded an excellent view of the main street of Little Pine. The rancher had secretly installed himself there earlier in the day and had been watching the comings and goings below closely with growing concern. Alarm bells first rang for him when he saw the Texans emerge with a determined-looking Dooley armed with a shotgun. King had never figured on the old drunk taking a hand in things and it suddenly seemed to narrow the odds considerably.

When he saw the sheriff disappear down the side alley of Kate's Place after a brief consultation with the others, he guessed that the wily badge-toter was aiming to get the drop on the occupants from the rear. Only the bravest or most foolhardy of men would risk being caught in crossfire, especially when one of the weapons involved was a powerful scatter-gun.

As the seconds ticked away, King waited for the inevitable roar of gunfire, teeth gritted and fists balled, almost as if it was directed against him. But still, when it finally came, he gave a visible start and turned pale. Already an icy premonition filled his heart. It was no surprise for him to see two familiar figures back out of the doors towards their horses before mounting up and galloping off. No doubt the sheriff had advised the Texans to leave town as quickly as possible — if such advice were needful.

However, contrary to what might have been

expected, he found himself neither enraged nor frustrated by this turn of events. Instead, it merely made him focus even more intently on the problem at hand. He now understood clearly that he had underestimated his antagonists. Getting these Texan troublemakers off his back would be a lot more difficult and costly than he had figured. But there *was* a way.

Together they were a formidable obstacle, but if he could pick off one, the younger one who was siding with the nesters, the other would have no reason to stick around any longer, never mind to take up the battle for a breed of people he despised. Sure he might go gunning for the *pistolero* who killed his friend, but that was neither here nor there. In the chessboard of King's cold and calculating mind, pieces could be ruthlessly sacrificed when necessary – the only thing that mattered was winning the game. But even Prescott on his own was a force to reckon with. Those damned guns he carried and the way he could handle them. But for every job there was a man. And King knew just the man for this one. . . .

CHAPTER 8

A few days after these dramatic events, Jim was surprised to find himself summoned by Nathan Jackson. As he made his way to the low, hacienda-style building where his employer lived, the Texan tossed over in his mind possible reasons for Jackson's request to see him.

Maybe with Bud Lewis dead and his two suspected accomplices also despatched hellwards, the rancher might reasonably have reached the conclusion that the worst of the trouble was over and Jim's rather expensive services were no longer needed. Or perhaps he was angry at Jim's mixing in with an argument that had nothing to do with the Zion outfit. But he didn't really entertain the latter notion very seriously; in his view, Jackson wasn't the kind of man who would hold it against someone for doing what was only right and natural.

He entered the cool shade of the enclosed court-yard with a fountain bubbling quietly in its centre. The men said that Jackson had originally come to the territory with a young Mexican wife and it was for her that he had built his ranch in the Spanish fashion – to prevent her being too homesick for her native land. Some maintained that the ruse had not worked and that she had left him to return to her family in a matter of months; others that she had been taken by cholera after a few years of happy married life. Either way, there were no wife or children about the place and Jackson lived in the rambling place alone apart from a few trusted servants.

Jim stepped on to the veranda and knocked respectfully on the oak door set in the white adobe wall. After a while a kindly old housekeeper admitted him and led him to the drawing-room where Jackson was waiting, dressed in unfamiliar city clothes. Jim was a little taken aback by this; wearing a well-cut broadcloth coat, with a silk waistcoat and matching cravat, Jackson looked more like a successful banker or politician rather than the plain and honest rancher Jim knew.

Jackson noticed the Texan's reaction to his appearance and chuckled ruefully.

'Don't mind the fancy duds none,' he said with a conspiratorial wink. 'It's still the same man underneath them. As you know, I've been East on business for the last few days. You gotta look the part for these city folk; if they figure you for a dumb hick, they'll fleece you of every cent you have.'

He paused and stood up, clasped his hands behind his back and walked over to the mantelpiece above which hung some gloomy ancestral paintings.

'I understand you had some . . . bother in town a couple of days ago,' he said, fixing his eye on these forbidding-looking portraitures.

'You heard right,' affirmed Jim, his mouth tightening into a defiant expression as if he was expecting some kind of angry reproach.

But Jackson merely reacted with a neutral nod, his mind seemingly on other things.

'And the upshot of it was that you and your partner plugged a few of Little Pine's better-known denizens.'

'If "denizen" means skunk, that's about the size of it all right,' Jim agreed, darkly.

'Hm,' continued Jackson. 'And it also seems that Sheriff Dooley assisted you in these proceedings as a back-up man.'

'That's true too, sir,' replied Jim.

The cattleman turned to Jim and for the first time the Texan noticed that Jackson wore an expression of approval rather than anger on his face.

This was confirmed by the rancher's next words.

'What you did was right, Langford. And, by God, if I'd been there, I swear I'd have backed you myself. But it does leave us with a problem.'

'What's that?'

'Dooley lit out following the showdown. I gotta give full marks to the old-timer for the way he shaped up, but after that his nerve just broke and he took off with all his gear. Likely he'll hole up in some border town and soak up tequila until his money runs out, then come crawling around to look for his job back, hoping all the commotion has blown over. He'll probably get it too; he may not be much of a lawman but he's the best Little Pine can do.'

Jim listened to all this in puzzlement.

'Well, what's this to do with me, Mr Jackson? You said yourself Dooley'll be back some day. And though it's a fact he wasn't very effective when he was around, he certainly came through for me and Wade when the chips were really down. I guess he's earned himself another crack at the job, but the town'll just have to decide about that when he shows up again.'

'But don't you see?' said Jackson, slapping the fist of one hand into the palm of the other. 'Like I told you before, there's big trouble headed toward this country – I can feel it in my bones. Morgan King's behind it in some way; he won't be happy until he owns all the land in these parts – including mine. Today it's the nesters; next it'll be the other ranchers. He'll swallow us all up if nobody stops him!'

Jim listened patiently to this outpouring.

'But I still don't know where I fit in to all this. What do you want me to do about it?'

Jackson looked at him intently.

'You may not know this, Jim, but some time ago the good folk of Little Pine elected me mayor of the place. Mostly it's an honorary title, but one of the few functions is to appoint the sheriff. I'm asking you to fill the post – at least until Dooley returns.'

Jim stared at the other man incredulously. Him a sheriff? It was like asking the Devil to have a spell at running Heaven.

'You're askin' me to wear a tin star?' he eventually stammered out in sheer disbelief at what he had heard.

'Yes,' said Jackson, eyeing him squarely. 'And it's my opinion you'd make a pretty fine job of it.'

Jim sat down heavily in the nearest seat, his head spinning. He'd practised quite a few trades in his restless life but never that of a guardian of the peace. The very thought of it was preposterous.

Jackson took advantage of his silence to press home his case.

'Think about it, Jim. Frankly I don't really need you here anymore – I consider our little rustling problem solved by certain recent mortalities. But the town needs you; if things start getting out of hand, that's where it's likely to happen. I owe a debt of duty to the citizens to protect them from lawlessness; you owe it to your friend to stick around and face up to the trouble that is surely coming as a result of your recent actions. The solution is simple: accept the post.'

Through his swirling thoughts, Jim perceived the truth of what his employer was saying. If he wanted to stay on and help his partner, it would be the best – the only – thing he could do. He felt he was being more and more drawn into a situation that was beyond his control but he could see no way out.

Except, of course, the simplest: to get up on his horse and ride out, without ever looking back. No one would blame him for it – only himself. But then there was no tougher judge than his own innate sense of honour and self-respect. Seen in this light, there was really no choice. He shook his head with an air of weary disbelief, as if he could hardly credit the words he was about to utter, the words of a dang fool entrapped by his own impossible ideals of duty and friendship.

'OK, I accept,' he said finally. And for some reason, it felt like he had just heard himself announce his own death sentence.

It would take some while for Rachel to recover from the physical and mental trauma of the attack upon her by Bull and Scarecrow. During that time, Wade found himself acting as confidant to the distressed woman and this closeness of relationship caused their intimacy to grow apace.

He hadn't said much about the action he had taken concerning the perpetrators of the outrage against her but she gathered it had been both drastic and permanent. She hesitated to enquire too closely as to the details; it entailed a side of him she knew little but feared much. However she divined that, underneath his easygoing exterior, there lurked a different kind of man, capable of sudden and extreme violence. And though she knew that he would never turn that violence on the weak or those

he cared for, it didn't stop her dreading that unfathomable depth in him. She sensed also that it was
somehow tied in with and reinforced by his friendship with Jim and it was with him that she would have
to battle for the young cowboy's soul. For by now she
was hopelessly in love with this enigmatic man who
could be so kind and gentle to those he favoured, yet
so savage with his enemies.

Late one night, after Seth had gone to bed, Wade
and Rachel were sharing a coffee by the dying
embers of the fire when she finally got to ask him a
question that had been intriguing her for some time.

'How did you and Jim meet?'

The query was posed in a casual, small-talk kind of
way but behind it there was much pent-up emotion
and suspense. Despite their ever-increasing closeness, she felt there was some obstacle between them,
like a hard, immovable stone. If his acquaintance
with Jim Langford was part of this obstacle, she was
determined to understand it better in order to
remove it from the path to the heart of the man she
loved.

Wade had been sitting gazing a little dolefully at
the flickering flames that danced in the wrought-iron
grate, and looked up right away, a hint of suspicion
in his eyes. From long habit he was wary of personal
questions, especially as there were a few phantoms in
his past he was not particularly keen to let walk again.
But when he beheld Rachel's wan, beautiful face, still
bruised from her recent brutal experiences, and the

pleading look in her lustrous eyes, he felt his natural reticence melt away like frost before the sun. Here was a woman who had been shockingly hurt and abused, a woman who was pulling herself together with a toughness and determination he admired, a woman whose every concern seemed directed not towards herself but others, like her brother and himself. He couldn't withhold anything about himself from such a person, no matter how private or painful; he knew he could trust her with his very life. As Rachel watched him anxiously, the frown faded from his face to be replaced with an assenting smile, then his brow knit again, however this time not in perplexion but in remembrance.

'I must have been about sixteen when I started cowboyin'. My folks got carried off with the scarlet fever when I was still a baby and I was brung up by relatives. They did the best by me as they saw it, but there was never any real fondness there and I quit their keeping just as soon as I was able. We lived in a small town and I used to see drovers come in off the trail if a cattle-drive was passin', dusty, sunburned, saddle-worn but always full of life and fun. I was taken by the way they stuck together too, like one big, happy, noisy family. Maybe I envied them for that, felt it was something I wanted to belong to as well – I don't know. But I hit the road with the first drive that would hire me and never looked back since. The hours were long and the wages low, but there's something about the life, the freedom, the friendship. . . .

'Anyway, a few years on, somewhere on the Goodnight-Loving trail, a new hand joined the crew. He was older than me, more experienced, a lot savvier. But somehow we seemed to hit it off right from the beginning. In a way, I think I reminded him of himself when he was my age, if that makes any sense. At the end of the drive, we decided to ride together and that worked out well – or did until a while ago.'

Wade paused, as if coming to the crucial part of the story.

'I always knew that Jim was different from the other rannies. He kept himself to himself, never got dead drunk like the everybody else – though he was no killjoy either – and never wasted his time or money on any frivolous thing; in fact always seemed a mite on the serious side. I guess I was the only real friend he made all the time I ever knew him. But if a man's got one real friend, I reckon it's worth ten false ones.

'Anyway, Jim used to disappear quite regular and one day, out of sheer devilment, I tailed him. He fetched up at a dry creek, looked around him care-ful-like, then unpacked something he had in his saddle-bag. I was real surprised when I saw it was just some old tin cans the cook must have thrown out sometime. He set them up on some rocks, walked off and then turned around lightning fast, drew out his gun and let the lead fly. He was pulling the trigger so fast he made six shots sound like one, and boy, did he make those tin cans dance! I don't think a single shot missed and his Colt was back in its holster before the last can hit the ground.

'I was so impressed by this fancy marksmanship, I couldn't avoid lettin'out a holler to him and found myself lookin' down the barrel of his pistol. My blood ran cold when I saw his face, for it was stern and hard, like it was carved out of a rock, and for second, I thought my last hour had come. But when he saw it was me, he looked kinda foolish and holstered up. But he was pretty mad too.

' "Damned jackass!" he shouted at me, "Coulda' got yourself killed. Never sneak up on a man that's usin' a gun; sure way to get a bullet in your brisket".

'But he calmed down after that when I pleaded with him to show me how to use a revolver the way he did; he gave in, though reluctant-like.

'So from then on we got to practising often as time allowed, and before long I was near as good as him, not as accurate, but maybe a shade faster.

'He never talked much about his past, but I figured from the little he'd said that he'd been on the wild side as a youngster, learnt how to fend for himself the hard way and ended up using his prowess with a pistol to make a living. Eventually he got sick of that kind of work and decided to try a more peace-able existence as a cattle-herder, though he still liked to try out his old skills every now and again – but this time with tins rather than targets that could shoot back.

'Around that time we began to talk a lot about maybe running our own place one day, just a small ranch with a few head that two partners could handle. But even that costs some and I always figured it for a pipe dream to while away the hours around a camp-fire of an evening.

'But then one day he came to me with a proposition. Said he'd heard about a job up north for men handy with a gun, the kind of job that might make us enough money to put down a deposit on a small ranch, start raisin' our own cattle instead of baby-sittin' someone else's. At first I wasn't keen. I was happy enough doin' what I was doin'. The venture Jim was proposing sounded like a big gamble – the stakes being our own lives and liberty if the business turned bad. But Jim kept workin' on me and, in the end, I agreed to go along with him to at least find out some more about the deal on offer. Guess in the end I was just a mite curious to know more about it myself.'

Wade paused here and cast Rachel a strange look.

'Have you ever heard about the Johnson County War?'

'Nooo . . .' answered Rachel, puzzled. 'Was that part of the Civil War or one of the Indian Wars?'

'Neither,' replied Wade. 'Though probably just as vicious in its way. This war ended only months ago. Surely you read about it in the papers or heard about it in town?'

'As regards papers,' said Rachel tartly, 'I don't

know when I'd find the time to read them. As for town, I haven't been there in a year. It wasn't safe for me whilst King's men were. . . .'

Rachel's voice trailed away; a familiar haunted and hopeless look that Wade had come to dread entered her eyes. Hurriedly he intervened.

'Well, not so long ago, there was an awful lot of rustlin' goin' on in Wyoming, especially in Johnson County. The thieves were from all sorts of back-grounds includin' cowboys fired from their jobs and hopin' to set up a spread of their own – only usin' other people's cattle. Naturally the owners of the big ranches got fed up with this and got together to form a Stock Growers' Association. Their aim was to stop the cattle-stealin' problem – permanently. So they made up a list of the worst offenders and then set out to find the right kind of men to cut down on that list. That's where me and Jim came in. He heard about the job and talked me into takin' it on with him. The pay was good at fifty dollars a day plus a bonus of another fifty on every rustler killed.'

Wade hesitated here as he noted a look of distaste cross Rachel's face.

'That might sound a bit brutal to you, Rachel, but on the range takin' a man's horse or takin' his cattle mean robbin' him of his livelihood. Ain't but one answer to that and that's either the bullet or the rope. And for my money, the bullet's a mite faster and kinder.

'Anyway, we was hired along with about twenty

105

others – mostly Texas boys, and even got took on a special train from Cheyenne, along with ponies, guns, ammo and enough dynamite to blow Johnson County to kingdom come. Heck, we even had a doctor along with us to look after any man that got wounded. Yessiree, we were like a real army with a proper commander – an ex-Union Army officer called Major Frank Wolcott. We called ourselves the Regulators – for we were out to regulate the hash of any scallywags and rogues around the place.

'We got into Casper, at the end of the line, about three in the morning. First thing we done then was cut the telegraph wire to Buffalo – the only main town around – so that no one would know we were comin'. Major Wolcott had a list of over seventy names in his pocket, all known cattle-thieves, and the time had come to start whittlin' it down. On the first night, during a stopover along the way, we heard word that two jaspers by the name of Nate Champion and Nick Ray were wintering in an old line-shack on the KC range. When Wolcott looked up his list, both men's names were on it. From that moment on their fate was sealed.

'It was a bitter cold April morning when we arrived at the KC. We surrounded the cabin and waited for someone to appear. Eventually an old man opened the door and stepped out. He was carrying a bucket and on his way to fetch some water from the river. Silently Wolcott made a sign not to fire. It was obvious that this wasn't one of the men we were after.

When he got close enough, we jumped him and dragged him quickly into cover. Boy, was he surprised! It turned out he was a fur trapper by the name of Bill Jones who'd just stopped by with a friend to visit the men we sought. Wolcott ordered him held to prevent him warning the others and also to see if anyone came lookin' for him. Sure enough, the other trapper comes out in a while to see what's holding up his buddy. We bagged him too and then settled down to wait for the men we were really after.

'The next man to come out was totin' a rifle and we knew straight off he was one of our targets so we opened up with all guns blazin'. He fell to the ground and started crawlin' to the cabin with the dirt spittin' up around him from the lead that was bein' slung in his direction. Then an amazing thing happened: the door suddenly opened and a feller dashed out. He grabbed his wounded *amigo* by the collar and hauled him into cover inside. It was done so fast and so surprised the boys by the sheer courage of it that they plumb forgot to fire. That *hombre*'s handle was Nate Champion and, as he showed by this and his other actions, no man better deserved his name.

'Nate and Nick must have realized that they'd never get out of that particular scrape alive. Not that it mattered particularly to Nick; he was beyond caring and died of his wounds a few hours later. But as for of Nate, he intended to sell his life as dear as he could and killin' him weren't gonna be easy. The

Regulators kept up a steady stream of fire on the shack but Champion just returned the compliment and there was no safe way of getting at him so, despite the odds, it was gonna take a while. But, in the end, there could be only one result. We all knew that. Most especially Nate.

'In the middle of all this, a homesteader came ridin' by, along with his son who was drivin' a wagon. Once he saw what was happenin' he shouted to the son to get the heck out of there. The boy jumped on one of the team horses, cut the traces and the pair of them lit out like bats out of hell.

'Well, now the fat was really in the fire. As soon as those men reached Buffalo, they would raise the alarm on what was goin' on at the KC. And the sheriff there, Red Angus, was no friend of the Stockgrowers' Association. He'd waste no time in gatherin' a posse to come after the Regulators. And there'd be no shortage of volunteers either, for the big ranch owners were none too popular among ordinary folk. They were seen as having too much land and not enough manners.

'So Wolcott decided to hurry things on a little. He ordered an old cart dragged up, piled high with brush and set afire. Then four men pushed it towards the log cabin. Next he turned to me and Jim and said, "You men are the best shots in the outfit. Get round the back and cover that ravine about fifty yards off. My hunch is that when this rat bolts, that's where he'll make for".'

'Me and Jim looked at each other. We didn't much like the situation. Two men with Winchesters against one desperate fugitive didn't seem very fair. But we'd taken the money and made a contract. Now – no matter how hard – we had to honour it.

'Soon the hideout was well ablaze and some of the boys thought that anyone inside must be dead. "Reckon the cuss has shot himself", someone said. "No one could stay inside that hellhole one minute and still be alive".'

'But then we heard a shout. "There he goes!" And sure enough, a man in his stockinged feet and armed to the teeth came tearing out of the smoke at the back. Like the Major had predicted he made straight for the gulch but waiting round the bend, with levelled rifles, me and Jim were ready for him.

'The first shot we fired struck him on the gun arm and his carbine slipped from his grasp. He made a reach for a pistol stuck in the waist of his pants but another shot hit him in the chest, followed by two through the heart. He dropped to the ground, gave a few shudders, then lay stock still. Nate Champion, maybe the biggest rogue but certainly one of the bravest men I ever seen, was finally dead.

'All the others were hollerin' in triumph but me and Jim just looked at one another. We felt no joy in this killing. It felt more like a cold-blooded execution. Against such overwhelming odds, Champion never stood a chance. It was a wonder he held out as long as he did.

Major Wolcott must have thought the same. For, as he stood over Nate's lifeless body, he said, "By God, if I had fifty men like you, I could whip the whole state of Wyoming!"

'Meanwhile Red Angus had rounded up a posse of no less than three hundred men and was headed our way at a gallop. When we got wind of this, we retreated to a ranch in a place called Crazy Woman's Creek. Some of us got up a barricade of sorts and then we settled down for a long siege.

'Well, to cut a long story short, we were stuck there for two whole days swappin' lead with those *hombres.* But now the boot was on the other foot and it was us who were outnumbered. We got a good taste of what Nate Champion went through and it weren't pleasant, I can tell you.

'At the end of the first day, the Major took me aside. "We're in a bad fix here Wade", he said. "We're outnumbered nearly ten to one and that posse ain't in a mood to take prisoners. Some of them are friends of Champion and they're mad as hornets. Our only hope is to summon help. I need some one to get out of here and alert the state governor as to what's happened. He's a good friend of the Stock-growers' Association and will ask the President to send in Federal troops. I know you are a man of cool nerve and an excellent horseman. Will you be our messenger?"

'It didn't take but a second for me to accept. I savvied it would be a dangerous game but it was even more dangerous to stay there doin' nothin'. The lives of Jim and all the others rested in my hands; I was determined not to let them down.

' "When do you want me to go?" was my only question.

' "Tonight", he replied. "Wait till it's dark, say two or three in the morning. Men become sleepy then, sentries nod off. Muffle your horse's hoofs and ride him real gentle until you're through their lines. Then sink in those spurs and go like lightning until you find the nearest working telegraph office. Remember, every moment counts".

'That night I set off through the brush, leaning low on my horse to cut down on my profile and ready to take off at the least sign of danger. But everything seemed quiet until I was almost clear and then a light flared up in the darkness near me. It was one of the guards putting a match to a cigarette. My pony was startled and reared up, letting out a snort of fear. I heard a curse, a shout and then the sound of running boots. That settled it for me; I gave a hard tug on my pony's reins and he jumped like a jack-rabbit before chargin' headlong through the scrub. There were shots comin' from every which way, a few close enough to singe my ears but we just plunged on into the night. I weren't wearin' no chaps and got scratched up bad by some thorn bushes but that was nothin' compared to a dose of lead poisonin', so I didn't worry none on that account.

'I don't know if anyone tried to follow but when we

got out of the brush, I couldn't see anyone behind us. Likely lookin' for a man at night was too much like lookin' for a needle in a haystack. So I made my way to Fort McKinney and got on the wire to the Stockgrowers' Association. Right away, they got in touch with the state governor who telegraphed Washington. Once the President was alerted to the seriousness of the situation and that an all-out war was about to break out in Wyoming, he ordered in the Sixth Cavalry. I agreed to go with them to act as guide and we arrived back at Crazy Woman's Creek on the morning of the 13 April.

'Turns out it wasn't a minute too soon either, for Red Angus and his men had constructed some kind of siege engine with a shield of logs in front to get close enough to the ranch house for to bombard it with dynamite. They'd just about got in range when a bugle sounded and the army came chargin' over the hill. For once the boys in blue arrived in the nick of time!

'There ain't much to tell after that. The cavalry took us all into 'protective custody' and there was a trial of sorts. But the trappers, who were the only witnesses to the whole sorry affair, mysteriously disappeared out of the county, either bought off, or scared off, or both. The case against the Regulators collapsed then and after a few months they had to release us and that was the end of the Johnson County War.

'I guess none of us came out of it with much credit

– save for Nate Champion. Heck, they even made up a song about him. Reckon he'll be remembered long after the rest of us is forgotten. And rightly too. For he died like a man while everyone else was runnin' around in packs like mad dogs, out for blood and not mindin' who got hurt along the way.

'So, out of work and out of pocket, me and Jim decided to come on back to Texas and lick our wounds. That's where we was headed when we came to this place. We thought we'd left our troubles behind, but I guess we just found some new ones here. Seems to be the story of my life.'

Rachel noted the sadness and regret in Wade's eyes as he earnestly unfolded this troubled history. She could see that he bitterly regretted his part in the whole shameful episode and also, in part, that he blamed Jim for involving him in something he would never have contemplated ordinarily. That was part of the problem that dogged the friendship of the two men. But now Rachel was also, unwittingly, a cause of that rift widening even further and she did not know what to do to help resolve the situation. Only time could sooth the raw scars of recent wounds. And whether they would have enough of that remained to be seen.

CHAPTER NINE

The stranger rode into Little Pine with a cold northerly wind at his back, ushering him along in a swirl of prairie dust and tumbleweed. Folk were too busy pulling down their hats and covering their mouths against the airborne grit to pay much never-mind to the latest drifter to hit town. This kind of weather didn't promote curiosity, for flying dust quickly blinded gaping eyes and choked wagging tongues. And the icy breath of the Rockies did not encourage the populace to stand around and gossip. So the new arrival in their midst made his way to Kate's Place relatively unnoticed by the scurrying townspeople. Except, that is, for one man who had good reason to be keeping an anxious lookout for trouble and sensed that it had just appeared in the lean, angular form of the tall horseman.

The rider looped the reins of his mount to the hitch rack and shouldered his way through the batwings into the drinking palace. It was quieter in here after the howling storm outside and, although the wind had been with him for the past several miles, he was glad to no longer feel its constant shove against his back.

Beating the dust from himself with a wide-brimmed black hat, he surveyed the saloon with a critical eye. It wasn't up to much. The sawdust needed changing, especially around the oversized spittoon where drunken cowhands had missed their mark. Overhead hung guttering oil-lamps, which cast an unhealthy pallor on the scene, for though it was the middle of the day, the grey, overcast sky let little light through its bleak canopy.

The newcomer let his gaze wander over his unsavoury surroundings. There weren't many in the place; probably few were so desperate for a drink as to venture out in such weather. A drunken Indian lay facedown in spilt whiskey at a table in the corner. Two seedy-looking townsmen shared a bottle at another. From their pasty indoor complexions, podgy bellies and timid demeanour, the stranger surmised that they were store clerks who had crept out for a lunchtime tipple.

His musings were interrupted by a voice from his elbow.

'Howdy, mister. Goddamnedest weather, ain't it? Real bad for business. Just as well we don't get that north wind too often or I'd have to up stakes and quit. If it was even a warm wind! At least then folks'd work up a thirst. Anyway, what'll it be?'

The stranger turned to the utterer of this speech

and examined him dispassionately. He was a short little man with greased-down hair, a greasy little moustache and a greasy little countenance to match. At that moment he was wearing an ingratiating smile, which slipped and fell from his face as he felt the other's leaden stare upon him. For, as he told anyone who cared to listen later, it was like looking into the eyes of a dead man and seeing in them your own frightened reflection.

'Make it a beer – cold as you've got,' ordered the stranger eventually, his voice harsh and grating like it was rusty from lack of use.

'Yessirree, coming up.' The barman scuttled away to draw the beer. He set down the glass with alacrity and was about to withdraw to the far end of the bar with the same considerable speed when the stranger grabbed him by the wrist in a vice-like hold. The 'tender flinched and raised a free arm, as if expecting a crushing blow. But instead his sinister customer addressed him in a soft, though somehow menacing voice.

'Where can I find Morgan King?'

'Mr King gets around a lot. I'm not just sure where you might find him right now,' answered the bartender cautiously, not sure whether the man before him might be a friend or foe to the rancher.

The stranger gave a humourless smile, then suddenly applied a savage twist to his victim's wrist, sending a searing pain up the hapless man's arm.

'What's your handle, *amigo*?'

'J-J-Jeff,' stuttered the bartender, his face contorted in agony.

'Jeff?' rasped the other. 'Sounds like a reb name to me. You a reb, Jeff?'

'No, sir. Not me, sir. I'm as true blue as Ulysses S Grant!' The man was pathetic in his desperate attempt to placate his tormentor.

'That's good,' continued the stranger, 'for I killed me a heap of rebs in the war. Kinda enjoyed it too. And you know what, Jeff? I can't see no good reason to stop either. Now, let's try again. Where can I find Morgan King?'

This time, completely cowed, the man stammered out the information required.

'He's usually at the hotel down the street about this time of day. He owns the place.'

The stranger held the barman's frightened gaze for a few seconds longer, like a rattler mesmerizing a rabbit, then he suddenly released his grasp.

'Thank you,' he said calmly, as if a perfectly normal conversational exchange had taken place.

Glancing around, he picked out a table less grimy than the others and sat down there, showing every intention of quietly finishing his beer as if nothing untoward had happened. Jeff, rubbing his aching wrist, retired to a corner to polish glasses sullenly whilst the two store clerks, having witnessed the little drama that had transpired, hurriedly paid their bill and took their leave. The drunken Indian was the only other remaining client and he was still dead to the world.

The pair of fleeing townsmen brushed shoulders with Jim Langford as he stepped over the threshold of the establishment, stopping for a second to adjust his eyes to the shaded gloominess of its interior. As his vision grew accustomed to the sombre surroundings, he spotted a dark figure in the most secluded corner of the far end of the room. Back against the wall, facing the door, he thought. It has to be him.

Taking his time, he made his way to the bar, aware of watchful eyes fixed upon him every step of the way. There he put both hands on the counter, well clear of his holster, and casually propped a boot on the footrail.

'Sure is ornery weather,' he remarked conversationally to the barman. 'Give me a glass of corn whiskey, and leave the bottle, would ya?'

With a nervous glance from Jim to the man behind him, Jeff hastily pulled out a bottle and poured the drink requested, then beat a hasty retreat to the back room. Something told him that it was no longer healthy to hang around that particular vicinity. He'd been a 'tender too long not to know when bad trouble was brewing and he'd had his share of it for the day.

Jim took a sip of the clear fluid and felt it burn a fiery path down his throat. But all the while his mind was on the man nearby, warily watching for his opening move. It wasn't long in coming.

'I thought you were dead, Langford.'

Jim set his tumbler down slowly and turned in a

118

leisurely fashion to survey the author of this remark.

'I don't kill so easy, Larrigo. You ought to know that better than most.'

Larrigo leant forward with a grim smile, eyes shaded by his black-brimmed hat. 'Yeah, I guess I just forgot. Come on over, and bring that bottle and another glass with you.'

Jim sauntered over and eased himself into a chair opposite Larrigo. Setting his drink on the table, he took off his own hat, wiped his forehead and put it on again, all the while aware of deadly gimlet eyes on him, dark and menacing as the double-barrels of a shotgun.

'And I heard you were rotting in some Mexican prison,' he said, by way of continuing the conversation.

Larrigo's face split into a white grin of amusement that had more of the wolf about it than the human.

'Looked like it was gonna be that way for a while. 'Cept the *Federales* didn't know who they were dealing with. They handcuffed me and sent me to the pen with an escort of just a sergeant and two privates. I killed off the privates real quick, but I didn't like the way that sergeant had been poking me around, so I left him staked out in the Sonora desert sun. Reckon his bones must be well picked clean by now.' Larrigo was propped back in his chair with an expression of dreamy enjoyment on his face at the memory of this gruesome revenge. Jim repressed a shudder of horror and took a sip of his whiskey, as if utterly unaffected by the grisly tale.

'So what brings you to these parts?' he asked, with an air of studied casualness. Larrigo snapped out of his reverie and fixed his questioner with a searching stare.

'Business,' he said finally. 'And you?'

By way of reply, Jim drew back his vest to reveal the tin star pinned on his shirt.

Larrigo let out a whistle of disbelief. 'You, a lawman. . . ? Well, if that don't beat all!' Then a sudden thought struck him. 'Say, do you know a *hombre* name of Morgan King?'

'Yeah, I know him. He the one that's hired you?'

'Mebbe, mebbe not. What's it to you?'

Unconsciously both men had tightened up and their hands had started to stray down towards their weapons. Neither was really aware of this, so intent were they on the interchange between them, but to any onlooker it was perfectly obvious that violent action was about to flare at any second and, from the look of both men, it could only be of the most lethal kind.

'Just this,' replied Jim. 'I ain't got no particular beef with King but he's lockin' horns with a friend of mine, a good friend. I took this job to make sure no harm comes his way. You savvy?'

For a few seconds Jim held the gaze of the man opposite, tense and dangerous. Both of them were bent forward, almost head to head, their postures mirroring each other's, with one fist resting white-knuckled on the table, the other clenched firmly on a gun-butt. For those few seconds it seemed that explosive action was imminent, inevitable. But then Larrigo slowly eased his hand off his pistol, his shoulders relaxed and he leant back in his chair.

'I'd like to oblige you, really I would,' said Larrigo, pouring himself a generous portion of spirit and swilling it thoughtfully. 'But you know what folks are like. Once they got a hold of a story they like to improve on it some – things get picked up wrong, exaggerated. First there'd be a rumour that you'd asked me to leave town real polite, next thing that you told me to leave town. Then someone would dream up some extra colourful little details; you'd beat me to the draw, say. Better – you'd then took my own pistol off me, whipped me with it over the head and had me beggin' and sobbin' for mercy at your feet. Now what do you think a story like that would do for my professional reputation? Who would want to hire a gunslinger who got his own weapon took off him and ended up beggin' for mercy on a bar-room floor? I'd be the laughing stock of every town I rode into. No, Jim, once I start a job, I gotta see it through. To the end. But there ain't no sense in us tanglin' just yet. Hell, mebbe this jasper King can't afford my services. I never killed man yet without a fee. 'Less he got in the way of my gettin' that fee, of course.'

Scarcely able to believe that his opponent had backed off, Jim held his gun-ready stance for a few seconds longer before he too relaxed and sullenly jammed his revolver back into its holster. He didn't like this turn of events. It seemed to be merely postponing the inevitable.

'OK,' he said grudgingly. 'But I'm warning you: if you hire on for King, we're gonna have to settle this sooner or later. And, if I have *my* way, it'll be sooner.'

So saying, he tossed off his drink, shoved back his chair and headed for the door. He had almost reached the batwings when he felt a sudden coldness come over him, like he'd just stepped from bright sun into deep shade. At the same time he heard a voice hiss his name from behind him. In an instant his hand was on his gun and he was turning, dropping instinctively on one knee. His finger was on the trigger, his eyes were seeking the target – all within the space of less than a second. But already it was too late. Something hit his chest with the force of a hammer, knocking all the breath from his body. He staggered and gasped, fighting to regain his wind. The room was swirling before his vision and all the strength seemed to have seeped from his muscles. The gun slipped from his grasp and clattered to the floor as he sank to his knees. Looking up, it was like he was sinking down a deep, dark well and at the top of it he could see Larrigo regarding him with sneering disdain, the pistol still smoking in his hand. He hadn't figured that the gunslinger would pull such a low trick as to catch him off his guard. Somehow he'd thought that professional pride alone would have ensured that his adversary would have given him a fair chance. His mistake was to imagine that the man he was dealing with had the same sense of honour as his own; now he was going to pay for that mistake with his life. He was going to die as he had lived, he thought, a goddamned fool. A bitter laugh rose in his throat that choked on the blood surging from his ruptured lungs. It was the last sound he ever made as he pitched face forward to the ground, gave one last spasm, then lay still forever.

That laugh nettled Larrigo. He'd seen many men die, a fair few by his own hand. Many had looked frightened as death approached, some surprised and others merely uncomprehending. But a man who laughed at the prospect? Something about that unsettled him. Although he did not fully understand it himself, the only real pleasure in his twisted existence was the power he exerted over life and death. Without that power, he was exposed for the miserable, empty effigy of a human being he really was. And somehow that dying laugh seemed a personal jibe that mocked him in the very moment of his ultimate triumph.

He turned to Jeff, who had rushed out at the sound of gunfire and was surveying the scene with shocked amazement.

'You saw it all, didn't you? He drew first; I had to defend myself.'

'I didn't see noth—' Jeff began to say, but catching the baleful look in Larrigo's eyes, decided it was wiser to play along. 'Yessir. I saw it all. It was a fair fight sure enough.'

Larrigo gave an approving nod.

'That's good. I'm sure Mr King will appreciate your help in this matter. And here' – he tossed a silver dollar on to the counter – 'make sure that Indian over there gets plenty more liquor when he comes around and he'll testify the same thing.'

He walked across the room to the body of the man he had just cold-bloodedly murdered and callously flipped it over with the point of his boot. He frowned to see the ironic smile still fixed on his victim's lips. He was not superstitious man, but somehow it seemed an ill omen, as if the corpse was party to some private joke of which he was the ignorant dupe. He pushed the perplexing thought from his mind and, bending down, ripped the star from the shirt of his fallen foe.

'To the victor belong the spoils,' he said, almost to himself and, shoving it into the pocket of his coat, he pushed through the doors and back out into the dusty hell from whence he'd come.

King was working on his accounts in his room at the hotel, the same where he had interviewed Jim and Wade, when he was interrupted by a knock on the door. Oddly enough, he rather liked this dry and monotonous task. For him, it was the equivalent of a miser counting his gold; he delighted in seeing his profit margins mount, even by a little. The figures, neatly laid out on the page in black and white, gave him a sense of progress and order. It was a matter of sore regret for him that people could not be so tidily arranged and manipulated as the numbers, rows and columns in the book before him.

Therefore it was with more than a little annoyance that he interrupted his task to respond to the importunate caller, imagining it to be one of his men looking for instructions on some mundane chore.

'Yeah?' he barked curtly.

'Larrigo,' came the reply. 'You sent for me, Mr King.'

The rancher's face turned from irritation to pleased anticipation as he strode over to unlock the door. Like most crooks, he had a morbid fear of being robbed himself and always made sure to maintain strict security.

Confronted with the sepulchral, dust-covered figure of the gunman, King blanched a little and involuntarily stepped back. It was like suddenly coming face to face with Death himself. Larrigo noted his reaction and gave a ghastly grin. He liked to strike fear into others; it gave him a power over them which he could turn to his own benefit. Fear, hatred and greed were the emotions he fed upon; the others were unknown to him.

He strolled into the room, his eyes boldly roving over its contents as if he were trying to figure out the worth of its owner. King hastily made his way to his accounts ledger and closed it shut, just in case the inquisitive stranger took it on himself to examine that, too.

Larrigo placed his hat on the table and took a chair then, setting his elbows on the rests and joining his fingertips together, he looked expectantly at King. His attitude was that of a businessman waiting to open negotiations on a commercial deal.

Feeling somehow that he had immediately been put at some kind of disadvantage, King hesitated for a second or two before he too sat himself down.

'Well . . . er, thank you for coming so promptly, Mr Larrigo. Especially in this weather. I haven't seen a storm like this in twenty years; must have been hell to ride through.'

'When someone asks for me, I don't waste no time,' Larrigo cut in coolly. 'Now who is it you want killed and how much are you willing to pay?'

'Well, really!' exploded King. 'Who said anything about killings?'

Rattled by Larrigo's all-too-blunt directness, these words escaped him as a reflex action. He wasn't used to such a frank admission of the ugly side of his activities; also his instinct was to deny anything illegal in case his utterances might one day put a noose around his neck. No, his way was innuendo, suggestion, inference; later he might need to claim that he was misunderstood, taken up wrongly, that whatever happened wasn't actually his fault.

Larrigo broke off the conversation to pull out the stub of a cigar from his vest pocket. Drawing a lucifer along the edge of the mahogany desk in front of him, he applied the resulting flame to to the tip, sucking on it until it glowed a deep red. Then he drew it from his lips to emit a silken stream of smoke, all the while fixing King with a searching stare.

'My business is killing,' he stated starkly. 'It's what I do best. And anybody that sends for me knows that or he's a damn fool. Now you don't look like a fool to me, although I could be sadly mistaken, so let's cut the horseshit and get down to cases. Who do you want gunned?'

A look of sullen resignation came into King's face. If plain speaking was the only kind of talk that Larrigo understood, then he'd have to break the habit of a lifetime and just tell the truth.

'A couple of Texan troublemakers,' he admitted gruffly. 'Name of Langford and Prescott.'

A sudden glint appeared in Larrigo's eyes, like a man who has just spotted an ace in his hand of cards. But, expert poker player that he was, he gave nothing away.

'I know Langford. We even rode together for a while. He's pretty handy with a gun. Cost you plenty to have him taken care of.'

The sullen displeasure on King's face deepened. This was going to be more expensive than he'd figured. He had hoped to hoodwink the gunslinger about the quality of his opposition to drive down the price. Evidently that wasn't going to be the case.

'All right,' he said, drawing out two tumblers and a half-bottle of whiskey from beneath his desk. 'Let's talk business.'

It was only after some hard bargaining that the loathsome pair finally reached agreement as to the value of two human lives. But eventually the whiskey bottle was empty and a deal struck. It was to be $10,000 for the demise of both King's enemies.

Then came the moment Larrigo had been waiting for. He leant back in his seat and viewed King with a shrewd, wry smile.

'I'll take my first five thousand now,' he said calmly.

King looked at him askance.

'Didn't we just agree that the money was to be paid only when the job has been done?'

'Well, that's just it,' replied Larrigo triumphantly, 'it's already half-done. I gunned down Langford 'bout an hour ago. So you already owe me five thousand.'

King looked at the other man in disbelief. But the gunfighter seemed to be completely serious: it was not some macabre joke.

'How do I know you're telling the truth?' he gasped.

'You'll find out soon enough,' sneered Larrigo. 'Go ask the 'tender at that flea-pit down the street. 'Sides, here's proof if any was needed.'

He produced the sheriff's badge that Jim had worn from his pocket and tossed it on to the table. King picked it up and inspected it closely. Sure enough it was the same old star that Dooley had worn for many years; even had a prong bent where the drunken old fool had once collapsed against a horse trough in an alcoholic stupor.

He looked back at Larrigo. The man was gazing at him intently and he felt a shiver run down his back. It was like he was being measured up for a pine box himself.

'I'll get the money to you today,' he managed to mutter eventually through a throat gone dry with fear. 'Where can I find you?'

'Seeing as how this is the only hotel in town, I guess you'll find me here,' rejoined Larrigo. 'I'll go stable my horse while you book me in. And I want the best room in the place, hear? On your bill, of course.'

King seethed at being treated like a menial servant. After all, Larrigo was *his* employee, not the other way round. But he controlled his anger, merely grunting a grudging assent as the gunman took his leave. But once alone, his thoughts raced ahead to the approaching resolution of all his problems. At last things were going his way. With Langford dead, there only remained Prescott between him and the fulfilment of his dreams. When Prescott heard of his partner's fate, he was bound to come looking for Larrigo. Then the killer would earn his exorbitant fee by finally ridding the valley of the troublesome Texan. Or perhaps it would happen the other way round. . . .

King stood up and went over to unlock the door to a cabinet on the wall opposite. From it, he took out a shining Henry rifle, checked its action and inspected its breech. He pressed it against his cheek and sighted along the barrel, pointing it towards some imaginary target. He was no mean shot himself, he thought. He would not make the same mistake as before of leaving it entirely to others to do what was required. This time he would finish the job himself and make sure it was done right. When the gunsmoke next cleared there would be only one winner, and that man would be Morgan King!

CHAPTER 10

Tidings of the slaying of the newest sheriff in Little Pine were brought back to the Zion range the same evening it happened by one of its hands who'd been in town to see his girl. The news was ill-received by the rest of the crew, for while they usually didn't have much use for agents of the law, Jim Langford had been a workmate of theirs and had gained their respect and liking in the brief time they'd known him. There was even vague talk of a lynching of the perpetrator of the deed and, late though the hour was by then, some were for riding in that very night to administer this form of rough justice.

Jackson, however, soon put an end to that kind of talk. He came down to the bunkhouse himself to reason with his employees. For a start, he argued, there was at least one witness who'd stated that Langford had been killed in a fair fight. Second, he was against mob rule anyway; it set a precedent for all sorts of lawlessness and arbitrary violence. And thirdly, he felt it only right to inform Wade Prescott,

Langford's closest friend, as to what had happened to see how he wanted to handle it. The men listened attentively to their boss and grudgingly accepted his counsel, but secretly many were for settling the score anyway, though they agreed to stay their hands for a few days to see what Prescott would decide to do.

At dawn next morning, Jackson mounted his horse to go out and break the news to Wade of the tragic fate that had befallen his buddy. When he got to the homestead, he was surprised to find it seemingly deserted. The mystery was solved, however, when Wade climbed down a ladder from the hay-loft of the barn with a rifle in his hand.

'Been watchin' you the last half-mile, mister,' he stated baldly, his gun trained on the newcomer. 'Now who are you and what's your business?'

The rancher and the cowboy had not met until that moment but, from his demeanour and accent, Jackson divined that this must be the dead man's fellow-Texan.

'I'm Nathan Jackson, Wade. Your partner, Jim Langford, used to work for me.'

'Oh yeah,' said Wade, lowering his carbine with an apologetic smile breaking out across his face. 'Jim said you were a good man. Heard you even persuaded him to take on the sheriff's job once Dooley lit out. He must like you powerful well to agree to that. Sorry about the welcome I just gave you; I was expecting some less friendly company.'

Jackson nodded understandingly, then coughed

and shifted uncomfortably in his saddle.

'Well?' said Wade. 'Why don't you step down and come inside, tell me why you've come.'

Jackson looked at the house but made no move to get off his horse. He preferred to break the news he bore to Wade alone for the time being, on a man-to-man basis and without the presence of others to complicate things. Moreover, for some reason it seemed more fitting to say it out under the open sky, where both men were used to transacting their day-to-day lives. Somehow everything appeared cleaner and simpler in the great outdoors and even the heaviest of blows a little easier to bear.

'There ain't any easy way to say this, Wade,' he began in a firm but gentle tone. 'I came out here this morning to tell you that your friend – and mine – Jim Langford was killed yesterday. I know it isn't much comfort but I want to say what a fine man he was and how much me and the boys at Zion got to admire him during the short time he was with us. We're all gonna miss him a lot.'

Wade looked away, his eyes fixed on the far horizon. His face showed little emotion, just a kind of emptiness that reflected the sudden numbness he felt deep within. It was like he'd lost a part of himself, for he and Jim had become so close that it often felt as if they were one person. Now a sensation of hollowness and desolation gripped him; he was at one swoop robbed of his roots and identity, for he realized that for him Jim had been a whole family embodied in just one man. Once again he had been left an orphan to brave a hard, hostile world on his own. For a moment the grief he experienced overwhelmed him, and it was right to allow that moment run its course. But when he looked back at Jackson again, his countenance bore an altogether different set. The sorrow had vanished and been replaced by an expression of flinty resolution.

'How did it happen?' he demanded tersely.

Taken by surprise at the sudden change in demeanour he had just witnessed, Jackson stammered out his reply.

'Well . . . ah . . . it was a gunfight with a man called Larrigo. The bartender swears it was all fair and square though. Jim drew first according to him.'

Wade's eyes narrowed as he heard the gunslinger's name. He seemed to disregard the rest of the account as if he just plain didn't believe it.

'Larrigo . . . Larrigo . . . yeah, I know about him.' Brow knitted, he was talking more to himself than to Jackson. 'Not flashy or well-known but fast, fast as any of them. Carries a Navy Colt and a back-up derringer. Jim warned against him – tricky as a rattler and twice as mean.'

Nathan Jackson stared wonderingly at the man before him. Suddenly the young cowpoke had assumed a more sinister guise to him – that of a professional gunfighter who had carefully committed to memory all aspects of potential opponents, on the off chance they should happen to meet one day.

In the case of Prescott and Larrigo, it looked like that day might have finally come.

'OK,' Wade's voice snapped like whipcord, shaking the rancher out of his gloomy reverie. 'I'm going to town to settle this thing. Are you coming, too?'

For a second Jackson hesitated. He wasn't sure what Prescott implied by these words. Did he mean settle the arrangements for Jim's funeral? Or, more likely, make arrangements for yet another? Either way, he felt duty-bound to see this matter through. It was as a result of his pressing that Jim had reluctantly accepted the post of sheriff, and now, because of it, he had wound up dead. Whichever way it worked out, there was a reckoning due to take place. And he had to be there when it did, no matter which way it went.

'Yeah,' he finally assented. 'I'm coming too.'

He watched as Prescott had a hurried conference with the still heavily bandaged Seth. Rachel was still recovering from her own injuries and confined to bed under the strict instructions of the doctor. Jackson guessed that Wade was leaving firm orders that she was not to be upset by the tragic news of Jim's death. She would learn of it later when she had regained more of her strength. Then the Texan strode to the stable, saddled up his horse and rejoined the cattleman as the duo set out on the trail at a steady and determined pace. No word was spoken along the way for everything that needed to had been said and now was the time for action.

*

Only when Little Pine was in plain sight, did they slow down to a more cautious trot and Jackson eventually broke the silence that had fallen over them.

'Let's stop here apiece, Wade.'

From the slight rise on which they stood, they had a good view over the main street of the town. All appeared quiet and normal here – but that is just what they would have expected anyway.

'Seems almost a mite too peaceable,' remarked the cattleman thoughtfully. 'Why don't we split up? I'll circle round and come in the back way, tie up my pony somewheres and have a quick look about on foot. Just in case there's any nasty surprises out there we should know about. I know you're aimin' to go up against Larrigo as soon as you can, but give me a few minutes to make sure I can cover your back.'

Wade nodded agreement. What the rancher said made sense. There was no advantage to charging in bull-headed to a dangerous situation. He still thirsted for vengeance against the man who had killed his best friend but he could afford to wait a few moments longer. And it would be a relief to know that the only opponent he need worry about was the one he could see in front of him, and not some hidden assassin lurking in the shadows.

The Texan sauntered his horse into town, keeping his ears and eyes open for any sign of danger. But nothing seemed more peaceable than that sleepy western settlement sprawled out in the noonday sun. It appeared the whole place was taking a collective siesta, though he had little doubt that from behind curtained windows and through the cracks of slightly open doors, many curious and frightened eyes were fixed on him – not to mention some hostile and hate-filled ones. But he just mosied on like a man with not a care in the world until he reached the building he sought, where he got off his pony, tied up its reins and penetrated through the sombre, glass-panelled entrance.

As he stepped into the cool interior of the funeral parlour, his nostrils were immediately assailed by the sharp smell of formaldehyde. He stopped momentarily, his eyes adjusting to the gloom that reigned within.

It felt to him that he had suddenly entered the netherworld itself and he almost expected the shades of the departed to rise up and greet him. But instead a sallow, lantern-jawed man, dressed from head to toe in black, materialized, seemingly from nowhere, and spoke to him in a low, unctuous tone.

'Have you come to view the deceased?'

'I reckon,' replied Wade uncertainly, not quite sure what deceased meant but figuring it was a fancy word for dead.

His companion silently led him to an adjoining room where a white sheet covered something laid out on a long table. The odour of embalming fluid had got even stronger and out back, Wade could hear the muted but steady hammering of unseen craftsmen as they fashioned a casket for their latest client.

The undertaker tugged off a corner of the shroud to reveal the clay-coloured features of the corpse. Steeled as he was to the sight of death, Wade let out an involuntary gasp of shock and horror. To see a man fall in the heat of battle, still to all outward appearance vital and strong as he had been in life, that was one thing; to witness this pale and shrunken effigy of his former friend lying stiff and ghastly in the claustrophobic confines of this stinking room, that was quite another. With the bile rising in his throat, it was only with the greatest effort that Wade was able to prevent himself from being violently sick. Noting his reaction, the undertaker hastily replaced the sheet over the ashen face of the cadaver.

'You were a friend or relative, I assume?' he enquired with stilted courtesy.

'Yeah, we were buddies all right,' answered Wade. 'I don't know if he had any close relatives; he never mentioned any.'

'Well then,' continued the other man smoothly, 'perhaps we can discuss some practical arrangements. I realize that this is a difficult time to think of such things, but there is the matter of the funeral expenses — the casket, the headstone, the burial plot.'

He looked expectantly at Wade.

For a second the young cowboy failed to understand what he meant but then light dawned on him and a vexed look entered his face.

'Hell's bells, I ain't having him buried here! There's only one place Jim Langford would want to be planted and that's in Texas.'

'Texas?' gulped the undertaker, considerably taken aback. 'But that's a long ride from here. In this heat the body would cook in the coffin.'

'He ain't goin' in no coffin,' replied Wade grimly. 'I'll sling him over his horse and tow him all the way. Just do whatever you need to do so as the body is ready to go. I'll be leavin' within the hour.'

So saying, with the other man still standing speechless, he turned on his heel and headed for the exit. As his hand grasped the doorknob however, a sudden thought struck him.

'If I don't show up,' he said, without looking around so that his expression remained mysteriously unreadable, 'see Mr Jackson about the funeral arrangements. But then you might have another client on your hands. Or more. The killin' ain't done yet.'

With these ominous words, he quickly opened the door and slipped out, glad to breathe again God's own fresh air and leave behind the oppressive atmosphere of the death chamber.

Wade lingered momentarily on the sidewalk before proceeding on his way. Jackson would probably need some more time to complete his reconnoitre of the town. And anyway there was one thing to attend to before getting down to the main purpose of his visit. He walked several yards up the street and entered Kate's Place. It was deserted save for a few of King's rannies who hurriedly paid their bill and slunk out under Wade's challenging stare. They still remembered him from the fateful night in this same spot when he had confronted Bull and Scarecrow; the faded bloodstains from the casualties of that affair were still to be seen on the wooden floor. Now only the hapless Jeff was left alone with his sole customer.

'What'll it be, cowboy?' he queried, in a voice he hoped was one of light-hearted unconcern, but which came out halfway through as a frightened, high-pitched squeak.

Wade gave him a cold look.

'Make it a whiskey,' he said tersely.

As his drink was being served, the cowpoke tossed a sudden question at the barman.

'You know a jasper name of Larrigo?'

Jeff started visibly and paled, spilling some of the liquor he was pouring.

'No! . . . Yes! . . . That is . . . sort of,' he stammered out, unsure how to play it. 'He was here just one time. Just the once, mind you.'

'That the time he killed Jim Langford?'

Jeff's face crumpled. So Prescott knew about that. Maybe he knew too that Larrigo had press-ganged him into the role of unwilling witness.

'Yes,' he said feebly. 'That's right.'

'Did you see it?' continued Wade in a steely tone, his drink poised halfway to his lips and looking intently at the 'tender.

'Well ... ah, that is,' Jeff prevaricated, torn between his fear of Larrigo and this equally tough young pistoleer badgering him, 'sort of.'

'What do you mean "sort of"?' persisted his interrogator ruthlessly.

'To tell the truth, I-I-I was out back when it happened,' blurted out the barkeeper, as he finally cracked under the pressure being mercilessly applied to him. 'I didn't see nuthin' at all.'

After all, the man in front of him seemed in a deadly mood and ready to kill anyone he suspected of having a hand in the murder of his friend. Prescott was the danger right now; he could worry about Larrigo later. Come to think of it, if he lied to this man, there might not *be* any later.

'Yeah,' he continued in a surer voice, prompted by these thoughts and the relief of having to simply state what was only the plain truth. 'When Langford first came in, they seemed to know each other and even had a drink together. I went to the storeroom to check stock and next thing I heard, Larrigo shouted out your friend's name and there was a shot. As I rushed back in, Langford was lying by the door with a bullet in him and Larrigo was standing there in the corner, the gun still smoking in his hand.'

In his mind's eye, Wade quickly reconstructed the story these pieces of information told him. Obviously

Jim had been on his way out the door when Larrigo had called him out, taken him by surprise and gunned him down without giving him any real chance of defending himself. It was what he'd expected but he had to be sure. And, somehow, he felt better for knowing the details of his partner's last few moments on earth.

He held the barman's frightened gaze for just a few seconds longer, searching in his eyes for any remaining vestiges of falsehood. But, seeing none there, he nodded grimly to show that he accepted Jeff's version of events. But he wasn't done with the man yet.

'You know where Larrigo is right now?'

'Yessir, at the hotel, sir,' jabbered Jeff, relieved at apparently getting off so lightly.

'Well, go tell him I'm in town and I'll meet him in the street in five minutes.'

Jeff opened his mouth to protest. He had no desire to see the gunslinger, who had previously terrorized him, so soon again. But then he noticed the look on Prescott's face and decided not to push his luck. Besides, Larrigo was probably expecting this confrontation, maybe even counting on it. Hopefully it would not be a classic case of shooting the messenger.

'Sure thing, Mr Prescott,' he muttered subserviently, taking off his apron as he emerged from behind the counter.

Left alone in the deserted saloon, Wade propped

a boot on the foot rail and looked at his drink, still suspended in his hand halfway to his mouth.

'To you, pard,' he said, to some unseen presence as he raised his glass in salute before taking a sip.

As he set down the tumbler, he thought he heard a soft laugh come from the direction of the door. He spun round with his gun already drawn and ready to fire, thinking that his opponent had arrived already to surprise him. But that was impossible. Jeff had only just gone. And besides, the entrance was empty; the noise must have been made by the batwings swinging in the wind. Yet that laugh was familiar, it sounded almost like . . . Wade shook himself to clear his mind and resolved to take no more whiskey. Now, above all times, he needed to keep a cool and steady nerve. Ghostly imaginings would not help that. With the firm and determined tread of a man who knows exactly where he's going and why, he took his leave of the place.

CHAPTER 11

Wade stepped out on to the sidewalk and glanced down the street. There, in the shade, a dark-clad figure lounged casually against a post outside the hotel. When he saw Wade, the man straightened up and lifted his revolver a few inches from the holster before letting it drop back. This was done without thinking; the reflex action of a professional shootist who had been in dozens such situations before and for whom to ensure that the weapon would draw without snagging was second nature; for him dealing out death was a workaday chore, like wielding a hoe or humping a sack of potatoes. Taking the life of another meant nothing more to him than that.

Wade looked around him. He felt overwhelmed by a feeling of the unreality of it all; this was no blazing battlefield with cannon-smoke and the cries of dying men. It was the quiet, sleepy main street of a small Western town. On the sidewalk nearby, a cat dozed lazily in the sun; further down the street two horses tied to the hitch rail outside the hotel patiently

144

waited for their masters to slake their thirst within; above a shop door, a tradesman's faded billboard swayed gently in the slight breeze. Only the complete lack of human activity in the street distinguished this scene from any average day in any average town in this part of the country. It seemed crazy to die a violent death in such an ordinary, peaceable setting. There was his own horse waiting patiently nearby; all he had to do was walk over to it, mount and ride away from this madness. Ride away and just keep going until he was back where he belonged, not here facing oblivion on the street of a strange town. What could be more sensible, more reasonable?

For a second or two, Wade dwelt on this reflection, then he shook his head and the feeling was gone, replaced by an irresistible impulse to meet head-on the grim spectre of destruction that threatened him. His fear of cowardice and dishonour overcame his trepidation in the face of death and suddenly he was ice-cool and dangerous, no longer a frail and mortal man but a gunfighter, as much an efficient dispenser of violence as the lethal tool he carried. The man and the gun were no longer separate but formed one piece – a machine fashioned for ruthless and remorseless action.

Wade wasn't aware of the change. All he knew was that the jitters had gone and he was thinking straight again. In an unconscious mirroring of his opponent, he too lifted his pistol slightly and let it drop back. Everything was clear and simple now. There was no choice, no option. He could only go forward, retreat was unthinkable. All doubt, all fear was gone and only the determination remained to exert all his speed and skill in the crucial contest ahead – and come out victorious.

As he stepped out on to the open street, he felt the sun burn down as though through a magnifying glass. Anyone with any sense would have stayed indoors out of the fiery midday rays that day. Even the rattler would have sense enough to seek the shadow of a rock to wait for the heat to subside before resuming its deadly quest for prey. But not so Man, supposedly the most intelligent of animals. Only he, through the deep-born urge of greed or revenge would defy the laws of Nature and go forth into that blazing arena of combat and risk his very life, not for food, or territory, or a mate as a beast might, but driven merely by an abstract notion in his head created by avarice on one side and honour on another.

As they got nearer the two men surveyed each other warily. Neither had seen his opponent before but each instinctively recognized one of his own kind. It told in the well-oiled rig and the dully gleaming handles burnished with daily use. The movement, the stance, the look – all betrayed the traits of a professional gunman. Neither had any need to question the identity of the man before him; the only relevant question was who, if anyone, would survive the inevitable duel that was to follow.

Of the two, Larrigo was the more experienced in this kind of play. When he judged the distance about right, he stopped and regarded his antagonist with a cold, calculating stare. Wade stopped too and for a long few seconds no word passed between the two men; there was nothing to say. They both knew why they were there and what had to happen next. The only sound was the persistent creak of that rusty billboard down the street apiece, still see-sawing monotonously in the merest breath of a breeze.

Larrigo had been in this situation many times before, for Wade it was still a relatively new one. The older gunfighter was in no rush to force the issue; he liked to pick his moment, all the while studying his opponent for any signs of weakness. If the man was nervous, it was a good thing to let him dangle in the air a little; the longer he waited, the more edgy the other man got, his palms got clammy, hands shaky, the sweat of fear might roll into his eyes, stinging them with temporary blindness. Such a moment would be the perfect time to strike.

'I guess you're Prescott,' he sneered, eyeing his opponent closely. 'Wouldn't want to kill the wrong man.'

All the time he took in the aspect and demeanour of the man facing him. He didn't much like what he saw. For this young buckaroo did not look like the nervous kind. Instead he looked tough, fast and mean. Still, Larrigo had met several like that in the past and left them bleeding in the dirt. What he had on his side was experience and cunning, the will to slay and the ruthlessness never to hesitate nor be moved by pity or rage. In a trade that depended on the slimmest of advantages, such attributes were of inestimable value.

Wade did not deign to reply to the taunts of his enemy. For his part he had no doubt that he was in the presence of the one who had killed his best friend. From the creased and sallow features of his countenance to the funereal blackness of his dusty outfit, this gent exuded an aura of evil and death. He reminded Wade of nothing more than a scorpion poised to strike, its loathsome body arched in a stance of venomous hostility.

'Yeah,' continued Larrigo, when his previous sally elicited no response. 'Reckon you're the *amigo* of that old-timer Langford all right. You know, he should have retired long ago. I coulda plugged him six times afore he even got his hand to his gun. Weren't even fun – killin' him was like snatchin' candy from a baby. I shoulda let him have it in the belly. Woulda been died a mite slower that way. Guess I'm getting soft these days – too kind for my own good.'

Still there was no response from Prescott. He just stood there, his face an impassive mask, saying nothing. Only the eyes were alive, boring like twin gimlets into those of his mortal foe. Nothing could shake this man, nothing deflect him. He was implacable. Like a harbinger of Fate that no one could deny.

This uncanny silence began to get to Larrigo. Why didn't the *hombre* say something? Anything? Why did he just stand there, waiting, watching? Suddenly – despite the heat – Larrigo felt the day go cold. With a start he realized what was happening. It was *him* who was getting shaky, losing control of the situation. He would have to make a move and make it soon before the nerves really set in and his co-ordination went, his hands started to tremble, his aim became unsteady. He still had one ace in the pack: he would be the first to draw; the advantage of the attack was his. He'd better not waste it, or he might never have another chance.

With an inarticulate yell he reached for his sidearm, at the same time throwing himself to one side to avoid any answering shot from his adversary, should he be lucky enough to get one off. But it was as if he had slammed against a wall he hadn't noticed till then, a wall that somehow became a red-hot poker jammed into his upper ribs. His own gun went off, but at nothing in particular, his finger merely pulling the trigger in some kind of reactive spasm. His free hand strayed up to his chest. Mysteriously it had gotten wet, soaked right through from shirt to vest. When he looked down with glazing eyes, he saw that it was covered with a thick red substance; surely it couldn't be his blood? Only then did he comprehend that he'd been shot – shot bad – and was about to die. The ground seemed to give way beneath him and he felt an inky blackness envelope him as if he were already sinking into his grave. His senses slipped away as a darkness closed in, and he could no longer see or feel anything but still, somehow, somewhere, he could hear a faint, weary, familiar sound. Even in his extremity, his brain sought to identify the source of the perplexing noise. It was like the wheezing cough of an old man, rasping, repetitive and irritating. His whole mind focused on this puzzle, seeking to blot out the overshadowing threat of extinction that threatened it. Then he had it; it was that blasted sign down the street apiece, still swinging monotonously back and forth, pushed by a wind that was indiscernible to any human being in the heat of that stifling day. Larrigo gave a slight smile at solving this puzzle; in some way it gave him satisfaction to solve this last, trifling mystery before facing a far greater one. Then, with a final involuntary shudder, he gave his up his soul and turned to die face down on the dusty main street of Little Pine.

Wade advanced toward his fallen enemy with his smoking Colt still in his hand. He'd seen too many 'dead' men spring back to life with devastating consequences to take any chances. But before he got far, he could see that the precaution was unnecessary. Larrigo's body was sprawled in a twisted, unnatural shape that no live man's would ever assume, like a rag doll cast carelessly aside by an impulsive child. The cowboy holstered his weapon and looked down impassively at his slain foe. He felt no exultation or jubilation at the sight but instead a curious sensation of emptiness. Sure he'd avenged the murder of his best friend and, incidentally, rid the territory of one of its less salubrious characters. But killing Jim's slayer would not bring back his buddy, nor would there be any acclamations for his service of law and order by disposing of one of its worst flouters. No, the only real satisfaction he felt right now was that of an unpleasant but needful duty carried out and the removal of one of the last barriers to resuming a normal and productive existence instead of the wearisome and destructive circle of killing and vengeance in which he seemed to have lately found himself inexorably trapped.

But even as he pondered these thoughts, a pair of baleful eyes was fixed upon him that boded ill for Wade's continued existence in any form, productive or otherwise. Morgan King had taken up his favoured position by the window of his hotel room which commanded such a good view of the main street of Little Pine and from where he had often sat observing the doings of the ordinary folk going about their business and dreamed of a time when they would be subjects of a mighty empire of which he would be the head. Those schemes had come to nought thanks to the untimely intervention of the young buckaroo from Texas who had so suddenly checked his growing power and wrecked the results of many years' careful scheming. But now had come the time of reckoning for this troublesome inter-loper. King would not now make the mistake of leaving the job to others; he would finally ensure results by doing it himself.

He had witnessed the whole drama of the duel below with dispassionate eyes. It didn't really matter to him that Larrigo had been the loser in that contest. That gent had already served his purpose and his demise was no loss. In fact, it meant that King came out ahead of the deal to the tune of the five thousand dollar bounty he would no longer have to pay his failed assassin if he had succeeded in his grisly task. Yes, things were sweet and he was about to make them even sweeter with a finishing touch to wrap up everything to his satisfaction.

He picked up his Henry rifle and carefully drew a bead on the still figure of Wade standing over his fallen opponent. The rancher was a good marksman who kept his skill by regular practice and his target was close and unaware of the danger. The shot should be an easy one. For a second he wondered what the young gunfighter was thinking as he stood there motionless, looking down at Larrigo's prone form. Was he reflecting on the fleetingness of life? Its terrible fragility? The meaning of it all? Or was he just enjoying the satisfaction of victory over one enemy before moving on to the next – which King well knew would be him.

Whatever was going on in his potential victim's head, King quickly dismissed from his mind. He was not of a philosophical disposition; it was not good business. For him, the main thing in life was to achieve his goals. And now he was about to make a move that should solve the last of his problems.

With the cold metal of the breech pressed against his cheek, he looked down the barrel of his weapon and gave a grim smile. Prescott was making it too easy. He just stood there in the middle of the street, as if lost in a reverie. It would be like shooting a duck in a fairground gallery. Easier, for a duck at least would be moving.

He held his breath and started to squeeze gently on the trigger. The first shot needed to count for, with a man like Prescott, he might not get a second chance.

The cowpoke had the build and swift reactions of a bobcat. Even if he was only winged he'd be off the street in a trice, and roles could be reversed, as the hunted started to stalk the hunter.

But King was confident he would not miss. He would take his time to make sure of it. His finger tightened inexorably on the trigger to the point when the spring must give, the hammer fall and an ounce of molten lead would be sent hurtling on its way to rip through flesh and bone and snuff out that frail flicker of light called life. But that moment never came. Instead he heard the imperious command behind him.

'Drop that rifle, King!'

For a second the cattleman hesitated, then he slowly began to comply with the order. However, just as the firearm was at about waist level, he spun around, pointing the muzzle at the direction from which the voice had come.

He got off one bullet but never got the chance to see the result of that effort for a lethal volley of bullets came in reply to his desperate move and stopped him cold in his tracks. When the smoke cleared, it was Nathan Jackson who was still standing, revolver in hand, whilst his opponent lay stone dead, his blood soaking profusely into the pile of his own expensive carpet.

Coolly, as if this were an everyday occurrence, Jackson put away his weapon and gently closed the hotel door behind him as he left. His work here was done and now he had other business to attend to.

When he reached the street, he found Wade still standing by the corpse of Larrigo, still seemingly lost in thought. But the young cowboy was not totally unaware of what was going on around him.

'I heard some shooting a while ago,' he said to Jackson as he approached. 'You wouldn't know anything about that?'

'I might,' admitted the rancher with a rueful grin. 'Let's just say I covered your back and you can scratch King off your Christmas wish-list.'

'Good,' replied Wade grimly. 'Now there's only one last thing to do.'

He abruptly turned on his heel as if to go.

'Where in tarnation are you headed now?' demanded Jackson plaintively. 'Surely all the killing's done?'

'Yeah,' replied Wade. 'But the burying ain't. There's only one thing that Jim finally wanted and that was to make it back to Texas. I'm taking him there now.'

Jackson stared at him in amazement.

'But that's a two day ride from here. In this heat, the body'll be putrid by the time you get there.'

Wade gave him a quizzical look. 'I got my good friend the undertaker to give it some treatment. It'll still be in good shape when we get there. Don't want ol' Jim's ghost haunting me 'cause he wasn't laid to rest in his native state.'

Jackson nodded in understanding. He knew how Jim felt about his beloved Texas and that it was the only right place for his grave.

'What about Rachel though?' he asked. 'What will I tell her?'

A different expression entered the eyes of the tough young drover before him. The harshness of sorrow and anger dropped from his features and he seemed to shed years as a gentler look stole over his face.

'Tell her I'll be back,' he said simply. 'I don't know when but I'll be back. Just tell her to wait.'

Momentarily Jackson was tempted to gain a more exact commitment from the tight-mouthed cowboy but wisely desisted. The man would not be rushed and needed a little time to mourn the death of his friend and mull over all that had happened in the recent tumultuous days. To expect any firmer a promise from him at the moment would be folly. Wade had given his word; that was good enough for Jackson and ought to be good enough for Rachel. Sorry as her plight was, she now had hope. A person could put up with an awful lot as long as there was hope.

'OK, Wade,' he said reluctantly. 'Have it your own way. But make sure you do come back. Rachel will be awful sore if you don't keep your word. Come to think of it, so will I.'

Wade made no reply but merely smiled at this stern but good-natured admonition. Then he turned his back on newly won friends and future home to set out on his final, sorrowful mission.

CHAPTER 12

The two horsemen recognized each other from afar but neither slowed down from the steady canter with which they approached one another. One was a short, thickset fellow, overloading his spavined and long-suffering mount with his hefty weight, the other of a wiry, muscular build, seated bolt upright in his saddle and leading a horse behind him with his free hand. This other horse bore a grisly burden slung across its back, covered with a blanket, from which only the arms and legs protruded.

As the riders drew abreast, they exchanged a look of greeting but said nothing, merely touching their hats as a sign of mutual respect as each continued on his way without uttering so much as a hello. Words were not necessary in this situation. Dooley knew Wade Prescott and guessed that the corpse on the other horse must be that of his partner. He surmised that Langford had been killed by some agent of King and that Wade was now taking his body back to Texas for burial. Given the nature of the young ranny, he was sure that the surviving Texan would never have left Little Pine without exacting the most terrible revenge for his friend's death – and that had to include King, the orchestrator of all the recent violence in the valley.

He felt sorry that Langford had become a victim of that violence, but there had to be a purging in that place, so strong was the disease of greed and hatred there, and in it the blood of good men had to flow as well as that of the bad. He was just glad that the killing was now over and he could return to make a clean start in a town cleansed of the evil that had blighted it for so long.

After his initial desertion, he'd come back prepared to play a fresh part in the struggle against that evil – in which he had himself had once played a minor part – but it looked like the two Texans had done his job for him. But never mind – he would make up for it. It would be his duty now to make sure that no one like King ever gained such a grip in the territory again. From now on, law and order would reign and, with the help of decent citizens like Nathan Jackson, Little Pine would once again be the centre of a respectable community. The frightened lawman had run away from that responsibility before, but when he'd eventually sobered up in the gutter outside a Mexican *cantina*, he realized that no matter where he went, a man's past had a habit of following him there to torment his uneasy conscience. And always the same principle applied: the only way to

handle trouble was to meet it square on and, if necessary, die with dignity rather than run away in
disgrace. He was prepared to do that now but, thanks
to the Texans, that sacrifice was no longer needed.

As regards Wade, he paid scant attention to
Dooley as he rode on his way. His mind was on the
long ride ahead to return his dead friend's body to
the place he loved. But he noted that the oldster
seemed to have shaped up some, looked clean-
shaven and neatly dressed for a change. Even seemed
to have acquired a new sense of pride and purpose in
his demeanour. He was grateful for the help the
lawman had given him and Jim at a key moment in
their battle against King's henchmen and didn't
blame the broken-down alcoholic for skedaddling
shortly thereafter. Hell, it was a miracle that he'd
scraped up enough sand in the first instance to hold
a gun on the crowd in Kate's Place the way he did.
Maybe the old blizzard would stay off the liquor this
time; if he did, Wade had the feeling that he might
make a half-decent law officer after all.

With a sudden thought he reached into his pocket
and drew something out of it. Pulling his reins
sharply, he came to a sudden halt and, twisting in the
saddle, he called out to the rapidly receding figure of
the former sheriff, who also stopped and turned his
horse around.

'Hi, Dooley, you might want this where you're
going.'

He tossed something bright through the air, which

the old lawdog caught with surprising adroitness. Then, without waiting for a response, the Texan turned, gave his pony a light touch of the spurs and continued on his way at his previous steady pace.

The sheriff opened the palm of his hand to see what the young waddy had thrown him. It was an old tin badge with a bent prong. Wade had noticed it glittering in the dirt beside Larrigo's corpse and recovered it as a memento of his slain friend. But now he had found a better use for it: one that he sensed Jim would have approved of heartily.

Something welled up in Dooley as he pinned it back on his chest. It was a kind of pride mixed with bitter determination. This time he would honour the star along with all it stood for and never give it up again. He owed that much to himself, to the town, and to the strangers who had helped him understand what it truly meant to defend what was right and just. Now he swore to himself that, for his part at least, he would never ever forget that hard and bloodily learnt lesson. It had been a long, arduous trail for all concerned, fraught with much peril and unexpected turns but now each of them, in his own different way, was finally going home.